Kindness

Kindness

A TREASURY OF BUDDHIST WISDOM FOR CHILDREN AND PARENTS

Collected and Adapted by **Sarah Conover**

Illustrations by **Valerie Wahl**

"The Little Light of Mine Series"

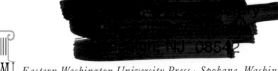

EWU P·R·E·S·S *Eastern Washington University Press · Spokane, Washington · 2001*

Library of Congress Cataloging-in-Publication Data

Kindness: a treasury of Buddhist wisdom for children and parents / collected and adapted by Sarah Conover; illustrations by Valerie Wahl.

      p. cm. -- (The little light of mine series)

Includes bibliographical references.

ISBN 0-910055-67-x (alk. paper)

  I. Buddhist Stories, English. (I. Buddhist stories. 2. Jataka stories.) I. Conover, Sarah. II. Wahl, Valerie, ill. III. Series.

BQ1032.K56 2000

294.3'8--dc21

00-048417

This book is dedicated to those immeasurably dear to me: family and friends

_____

Said Ananda, the Buddha's chief disciple, "Half of the holy life, Buddha, is good and noble friends, companionship and association with the good."

"Not so, Ananda," replied the Buddha, "all of holy life is friendship, companionship and association with the good."

Contents

My true religion is kindness.

— The 14th Dalai Lama

To the Young Reader

One day, as the Buddha journeyed alone, he stopped under a shade tree beside the road to rest and meditate. When the next traveler came along, he was so impressed by the extraordinary peacefulness of the Buddha that he stood awestruck before him. "Sir, who are you?" the man asked. "Are you changing into some kind of god?"

"No sir, I'll not become a god," replied the Buddha. Still, the man studied him closely and was not yet convinced.

"Well then," queried the traveler, "you'll become a wizard then?" Again, the Buddha answered no. "Are you only a man?" asked the traveler. The Buddha shook his head no to that as well. "Then just exactly what will you become? Who are you?"

"I am a Buddha, I am awake." [1]

This is a book of sayings and stories about the Buddha and his teachings, collected during the thousands of years since he lived. And just as the Buddha described—he was not a god, he was simply awake. The word Buddha means just that: the Awakened One. This particular kind of wakening has also been called enlightenment; it is the aim of the people who follow the teachings of the Buddha.

Siddhartha Gautama, known later as the Buddha, was born a wealthy prince around the sixth century B.C.E.[2] in a region that is now part of Nepal. Although his mother died soon after his birth, he lived a happy and privileged childhood in the palace of his father and stepmother. Because of a prophecy that he would someday abandon his father's kingdom, he was not allowed outside the palace compound. Hence, ease, comfort, and the gratification of every wish were all Siddhartha knew.

However, a time came when Siddhartha felt he must see the world beyond the palace walls. In secret, he traveled to the nearby city. There, for the first time, he witnessed appalling suffering, poverty and illness. Haunted by this experience, he had to know if it were possible for people to be free from such suffering. And so at twenty nine years old, Siddhartha abandoned his family and riches. He clothed himself in rags, left his kingdom behind, and set off on a spiritual quest.

He lived as a homeless beggar. He trained with various teachers, meditated, and reflected deeply on life and death, happiness and suffering. He became knowledgeable in the religious philosophies of his time. He also practiced severe asceticism, nearly starving himself to death, in an effort to forget the comforts of the world. Finally, convinced that there must be a middle-way to live the holy life—something between punishing the body and indulging every desire—he stopped his search. Six years after forsaking his kingdom, Siddhartha sat beneath a tree and vowed to stay until he became enlightened. The legend says that the very next day, just as the morning star appeared, Siddhartha became a Buddha. He found the truth he had sought, and felt that at last he understood the keys to human suffering and happiness.

Soon after, he began to teach others what he had learned. He was no longer called Siddhartha, but known now as the Buddha, the Awakened One. In essence, the Buddha said that he taught just two things—the cause of suffering and the end of suffering. He attracted a large following of both men and women during his lifetime. But the Buddha saw himself only as a guide, not a god. He insisted that each person test the soundness of the teachings for him or herself. By our own efforts, said the Buddha, each of us has the capacity to be enlightened too—awake, joyful and at peace with the world.

In the Buddhist stories and sayings that follow, wisdom and compassion are the threads that tie the stories one to the other. Wisdom and compassion are difficult to understand—that's why we use stories to show what they are. Learning to live a life based on these qualities is essential Buddhist practice. Meditation, the ancient tradition of developing insight and calming the mind, is one of the main ways Buddhists try to develop these qualities. They also believe that tolerance and generosity are very important.

This book is a collection of stories and sayings treasured in different regions of Asia where Buddhism took root over 2500 years ago. Many of the stories are funny and surprising. You might find you're sometimes puzzled and need to think about their meaning. The sayings between the stories are the wise words spoken by the Buddha or a teacher of Buddhism.

There are two kinds of stories: anecdotes and fables. Anecdotes convey kernels of Buddhist philosophy in a short story. Sometimes the teacher in the story is the Buddha; sometimes the teacher is a Buddhist monk or nun. Are these stories always true? Could they really have happened exactly as they've been told over time?

The other stories in this book are fables from the *Jataka*: perhaps the oldest and largest collection of folk tales in the world. Originally from regions of India, over time these stories blended with the teachings of the Buddha. The stories became part of Buddhist scripture. The hero in each *Jataka*—whether animal or human—came to be seen as the Buddha in a former life, working his way towards enlightenment.

Buddhists believe there is a close connection between all forms of life; be it human, bird, or flower. They believe in a life and death cycle that spans many lifetimes. The Buddha said that life is so deeply interwoven that over the ages, over time, each of us has been the other's parent. He taught that the separation we often feel between ourselves and other living things is an illusion—a kind of dream—from which we can awaken, just as he did.

Did the Buddha, the Awakened One, once live as a great ox and befriend an old farmer? Did a wise quail try to save the lives of his flock? Are kindness and compassion feelings we share with all living creatures? Could some of the *Jataka* tales really be true? Maybe. See what you think.

Preface

This anthology is a read-aloud book. In compiling these stories and sayings I hope to reach several different audiences. First, my goal is that this book be meaningful and broadening to parents and children of diverse faiths interested in learning from one of the world's great treasuries of wisdom. Second, this book is written with the aim that Buddhist families may read these stories and sayings many times, over many years. Finally, this anthology is intended to be a resource for the educator trying to convey more than a textbook sense of Buddhism to K-12 students studying geography, world history, or world religions.

Often the great store of wisdom and insight inherent in religion is taught to young people in the abstract. In that form, often the heart and sentiment of the issues addressed—the way each human being has found to respond to the great problems of life—can be lost. But a story brings to life characters as well as important matters. From its very beginning, Buddhism has had a long-standing tradition of story telling to convey and clarify aspects of its philosophy. The Buddha did not write down any of his teachings. His teaching was imparted solely through conversations, story telling and discourses—many of which he encouraged his monks and nuns to commit to memory.

Kindness: A Treasury of Buddhist Wisdom for Children and Parents contains several types of material: stories, anecdotes, wisdom sayings, and *Jataka* fables. My search for material was led by a desire to provide a broad sampling from a variety of Buddhist schools of thought and practice. Naturally, my search was also directed by what I believed children would be able to understand and enjoy. Most of the available translations of Buddhist stories that I believe Western youth will find understandable are from India, Japan and Tibet. Buddhist schools from China, especially the devotional traditions, are only sparsely represented. Certain other Asian countries with long-spanning traditions of Buddhism—such as Viet Nam and Korea—are also not proportionately represented.

Buddhism began to separate into various schools a hundred years or so after the Buddha's death. The two broad divisions within Buddhism are the Hinayana systems,[3] and the Mahayana systems.[4] These two systems are radically different in their philosophies. Nevertheless, there are some fundamental beliefs that all Buddhist schools share among which are the nature of suffering, rebirth, the flux of the phenomenal world, the nature of the self and the process of liberation.

Theravada Buddhism, the largest offshoot of the Hinayana branch, is often seen as "old Buddhism" and prevails in the south of Asia: Sri Lanka, Burma and Thailand. The son or daughter of Emperor Asoka (there is some dispute which), brought the Theravada teachings to Ceylon about 240 B.C.E. where they were at last written down in their entirety. There are three divisions of the Theravada Canon or *tipitika* (ti means three and pitika means basket). The name *tipitika* derives from the fact that the original was written down on palm leaves with a pointed steel tool; ink from berries was rubbed over the "page" and then delicately removed, leaving the dye in the indentations. These palms leaves were not formed into books, but were carried around in three separate baskets: one for suttas (sermons and discourses, including the *jatakas*), one for vinaya (rules for monks and nuns), and one for abhidhamma (commentaries). Known as the Pali Canon, these collected teachings were the foundational scriptures of the Theravada School and the only complete collection of scripture from the first 500 years of Buddhist history. From Ceylon, the Pali Cannon passed back to much of the rest of Southeast Asia—hence the Theravada School is also often dubbed the "southern school" of Buddhism.

A selection of fables from the collection of 547 *Jataka* tales of the Pali Canon forms a significant part of this anthology. As Buddhism interwove with Indian culture during its first 500 years, Buddhist monks and storytellers infused the ancient, Indian folk stories with the new teachings. The word *jataka* means birthlet or birth story. The hero in each story—whether animal or human—was seen as the Buddha in a former life, on the long road to enlightenment. The *Jataka* has been called one of the world's great ballads on the theme of the ascent of man: that willing the better, we will indeed become the better.[5] The *Jataka* tales now form one of the oldest and most complete collections of folklore extant.

The *Jataka* fables focus strongly on two major themes within Theravada Buddhist teachings; a deep compassion for all life, and karma—the consequences of good and bad action. Additionally, as the *Jataka* tales were ostensibly used by the Buddha to clarify points of philosophy, they traditionally include a "Story of the Present:" that is, a situation for which the Buddha wants to offer a solution and thus uses a Jataka tale to point the way. I have kept to this tradition.

Broadly speaking, the second 500-year period of Buddhist history is characterized by a profusion of literature from the Mahayana systems. Unfortunately, much of the written scripture from this early time did not survive intact throughout the ages.

Nevertheless, Mahayana is the branch of Buddhism that prevailed in India, then moved through Tibet into China, the Korean peninsula and Japan. Hence it is known as the "northern" school of Buddhism. The Tantrayanic and Zen schools within the Mahayana tradition include much written material but often need an initiated master to properly explain it. Nevertheless, humorous anecdotes and "crazy wisdom" stories abound and proved to be a great source for this anthology.

Throughout its history, Mahayanic Buddhism has developed and expanded. This situation has led to a profusion of "canonical literature." Particularly challenging for the person searching for the core teachings of the various schools within its traditions, is the fact that there is not one finally definitive, authoritative text. Canonical literature in the Mahayana traditions range from thousand-year-old Zen sutras to mystical Tibetan sutras. And further, because each person has the potential of awakening—of Buddha-hood—there is canonical authority given to words uttered from teachers (other than the Buddha) who are also considered enlightened. A number of the stories and sayings of this anthology include the wise words of these Buddhist teachers.

I have attempted to keep the canonical authority (when it exists), and vitality of the stories and sayings intact. At times in the retelling I have made revisions of awkward and archaic language. I have also drawn out the dramatic tension of a story whenever I thought it possible to do so without damaging its authenticity and theme. Also, I have associated each story and fable with a saying attributed to the Buddha or to a teacher of Buddhism. The stories and sayings are not always from the same schools of Buddhism, but juxtaposed, I hope to create a sense that there are some commonalties between very different systems of Buddhist thought.

The representation of women in the traditions of Buddhism should also be touched upon. But for some notable exceptions—primarily in the Tibetan tradition—it is quite difficult to find canonical material that represents women well. Consequently, I've offered only a few stories featuring women. Buddhism has been a patriarchal religion. Fearing that it would disrupt the spiritual focus of the monks, the Buddha was quite reluctant to have women become part of the monastic community. But under pressure from his own stepmother as well as his chief disciple, Ananda, the Buddha eventually relented and allowed women to form communities of nuns. His was a radical decision for those early times. Nonetheless, the effects of a male-led religion are only now, very early in the 21st century, beginning to be redressed as Buddhism grows roots outside of Asia. It is my sincere wish that future Buddhist story collections will include many more stories of wise, female teachers. In the meantime, as you read these stories aloud, please feel free to change the genders.

Within the ancient *Jataka* fables, as in the other stories of this anthology, are characters of all shapes and size that inevitably glean a bit of insight. But just as in life, wisdom doesn't often come painlessly. Children and parents of today will easily recognize within themselves the array of foibles and virtues depicted. That this recognition is possible is a testament to a body of teachings that still addresses the basic challenges faced by each individual, no matter the century nor the place.

1 From "The Book of the Fours" in the <u>Angutara Nikaya</u>. London: Pali Text Society.
2 Before the Common Era
3 The term Hinayana, "Small Vehicle" (for crossing the stream of suffering), was introduced by the Mahayanins. It is used here in the non-derogatory sense as a collective name for all pre-mahayanic schools of which the Theravada (School of the Elders) is the most significant. See H. W. Schumann's <u>Buddhism: An Outline of its Teachings and Schools.</u>
4 Scholars also distinguish a third, distinct system called Tantrayana. But because philosophically Tantrayana builds on the Mahayana, I have placed it under the latter's system.
5 Davids, Caroline A.F. Rhys, translator and editor. <u>Stories of the Buddha: Being Selections from the Jataka</u>

Stories and Sayings

Why look for truth in distant lands?
Seek it in the depths
Of your own heart.

Birdsnest

 Long ago in China, there lived a monk who perched in a certain tree every day to meditate. No matter if the tree swayed in fierce winds and rain, the monk settled himself comfortably, high up in the tree. Because of this, he was nicknamed "Birdsnest" by the village folk nearby.

Many of these villagers passed beneath the monk while hunting or while gathering wood in the forest. And after a time, they grew used to the monk. Some began to stop and talk of their concerns with Birdsnest. They liked the things he had to say, and soon Birdsnest became known for his kind and thoughtful words.

After more years, the monk's wise reputation spread throughout the province. Visitors from distant cities hiked to the remote forest for advice. Even the governor of the province decided that he too would like to visit Birdsnest to discuss matters of importance. So, one spring morning, the governor set off to find him. After traveling several days, he at last located Birdsnest's tree in the dense forest. The monk sat calmly, high in the topmost branches, enjoying the warmth and the bird songs of spring.

Looking up, the governor shouted, "Birdsnest! I am the governor of this province

and I have come a great distance to speak with you. I have a most important question." The governor waited for a reply but heard only the pleasant sounds of leaves stirring in the breeze. The governor continued, "This is my question. Tell me Birdsnest, what is it that all the wise ones have taught? Can you tell me the most important thing the Buddha ever said?" There was a long pause—just the soft rustle of leaves again.

Finally, the monk called down from the tree. "This is your answer governor. Don't do bad things. Always do good things. That's what all the Buddhas taught."

But the governor thought this answer far too simple to have walked two days for! Irritated and annoyed, the governor stammered, "Don't do bad things; always do good things! I knew that when I was three years old, monk!"

Looking down at the governor, Birdsnest replied with a wry smile. "Yes, the three-year-old knows it, but the eighty-year-old still finds it very difficult to do!"

All fear death,
All hold life dear.
Feel for others
As you do for yourself;
Remember this
And cause no harm.

The Mustard Seed

 Unlike the Buddha, Kisa Gotami grew up very poor. Her family had little food to spare. She often felt weary, hungry, and weak and so was called Kisa—meaning "frail"— Gotami.

When Kisa Gotami married, she moved into the house of her husband's family: the custom in India at the time. But because she came from a humble background, her new family treated her harshly until the day she gave birth to a child. She was respected now, with her new baby boy. Kisa felt proud and happy. Her new son was the light of her life. She cherished everything about him—his delightful laughter, his eager brown eyes, his toothless smiles.

But one terrible, tragic day, the boy was taken by a sudden illness. His death overwhelmed poor Kisa. She bundled him in warm blankets and held him tightly to her chest. Crazed with grief, she stumbled from house to house, begging for medicine that would bring him back to life. But instead of helping, people mocked her madness. "Crazy woman!" they jeered. "How can a person be brought back to life!"

Hours later, Kisa Gotami stood in the street, wretched and disheartened. As she wept over her child, a kind man passing by studied her. To himself he said, "This poor woman has lost her mind from sorrow. I think I know how to get her the medicine she seeks." He placed his hands firmly on her shoulders. "Dear woman, please let me help you. The wisest of men, a man named the Buddha, resides at a monastery nearby. I will take you to him and you can ask his advice. If anyone has medicine for your child, it is he."

He led her to the monastery where she found the Buddha teaching, at the front of a large group of monks and nuns. From the edge of the crowd she shouted, "Teacher, teacher! My name is Kisa Gotami. I am desperate! Please, my son needs your medicine!"

The crowd made way for Kisa to reach the Buddha. As she stood before him, he observed the child's lifeless face. "You did well in coming here for medicine, Gotami," the Buddha comforted her. "Here you will find the help you need. But first, before I can save your child, you must do something for me. You must return to the city from which you just came. There, find me a single mustard seed and bring it back."

Kisa Gotami's face lit up, for she thought this a simple task in exchange for her son's life. "Most important of all," said the Buddha, "the mustard seed must be from a family in which no one has died. Go now, make the rounds of the city and ask at every home. Bring me back just one mustard seed from such a family."

"Thank you good sir!" said Kisa happily. She turned and hurried back to the city. At the very first house she stopped and knocked at the door. An old woman answered. She easily gave Kisa Gotami a mustard seed—all India used them in cooking. But just as the seed was placed in Kisa's palm, she remembered the Buddha's further instructions. "Oh, pardon me. Before I take this, I must ask you, has anyone died in this family recently?"

The old woman's head lowered. She fell silent. When she raised her face, there were pooled tears in her eyes. "I'm sorry to say the answer is yes," replied the old woman. "My dear husband died six months ago."

"I am so sorry," said Kisa Gotami. "Thank you for your kindness, but I cannot take this seed."

A few minutes later she knocked at the door of a house with children running in and out of the entrance, chasing each other in play. A young woman saw Kisa standing in the doorway, and came to greet her. Some of the children stood behind the young woman's skirt to hear what the stranger wanted. "Can I help you?" she asked Kisa Gotami.

"I have been sent here to find special medicine for my son. I am looking for a single mustard seed from a household in which no one has died," said Kisa.

"We cannot help you. I am sorry. We lost our mother two years ago," stated the young woman quietly. "For many months I was so unhappy I didn't know how to go on." One of the boys reached up to hold her hand. She clasped his little fingers and continued, "But I knew I had to help my father take care of my brothers and sisters. That's what my mother would have wanted. I'm sorry we have no such special mustard seed for you."

And so Kisa Gotami continued to the next house, and then to another, asking for the single mustard seed. But always, someone had lost a beloved—a brother or a sister, a grandparent, an aunt or cousin, a mother or father. The list grew longer and longer.

After a time, nightfall came. People snuffed out their oil lamps for the evening. Kisa Gotami sat down, resting against a tree. She gazed down at her son in her arms. Studying him closely, she felt a gradual change in herself. Not a single household she had visited today lived untouched by death's sad hand. Many suffered just as she did now. She was not alone. And somehow, with these thoughts, her grief lightened just a bit, and she returned home.

The next day, at first light, Kisa Gotami readied her son for his funeral. Tears streamed down her cheeks as she wrapped him in clean cloth and said farewell. After the funeral, Kisa Gotami went back to the monastery to speak with the Buddha. The Buddha clearly saw in her face that she had come back to her senses. He asked, "Gotami, did you bring me a tiny grain of mustard?"

"No, teacher. I am done looking for the mustard seed. I know that in the whole city, in the whole world, there is not one family, not one person, free from the certainty of death. It is the way of all living things—we must at some time leave one another."

"And where is your child, dear woman?"

"At last I have said good-bye to him. I felt terribly alone in my grief, but now I know there are many others who have lost what they most cherished. We must help each other, as you have helped me."

Kisa Gotami, brought back to her right mind from her search for the mustard seed, became a very wise and compassionate woman. It is said that she never left the Buddha after her return to the monastery. And that from her experience, she was able to comfort many, many others in her lifetime.

Rest peaceful as an infant.
Rest tranquil as a waveless ocean.
Rest settled as a mountain.

The Elephant and the Wind: A Jataka Tale

 When the Buddha stayed at his monastery in Jetavana, there was a monk with a questionable past in constant fear of his life. If the wind rustled the leaves of a tree, or a shrill bird call rang through the forest, the monk shrieked and quickly hid under the nearest table. Soon, his constant trepidation began to affect the other monks. Not wanting to be infected with similar fears, the group of monks had just begun discussing the problem when the Buddha entered the room. Hearing all about the jittery monk, the Buddha gently suggested, "Don't be angry with this brother, monks. Once before, long ago in another lifetime, he carried this same dread in his heart. And just like long ago, with our help he will slowly learn to leave these fears behind." Then the Buddha recounted this tale:

Once upon a time, many years past, the Former Buddha lived as a Tree-Sprite in the jungled foothills of the Himalayan Mountains. And in those days, there lived a great, white, and beautiful elephant in a nearby city. The king gave over the care of his rare

elephant to the royal animal trainers, hoping that she would learn to perform tricks. Sadly though, and unbeknownst to the king, they treated her cruelly. Chained and shackled to a large post, she was held prisoner. They insistently barked commands at her. If she disobeyed her trainers or needed to rest, they prodded and poked her belly with sharp rods and lashed her legs with stinging whips.

Finally, they wounded her one too many times. Anguished, she fought against her shackles until they broke. With her immense strength she ploughed through the wide brick walls and escaped her compound. The trainers scattered and ran for their lives. The great elephant fled as fast as she could, deep and far into the hills. She ran and ran until she was very far from civilization. And still she kept running. The men who were later sent to recapture her found not a trace and eventually gave up their search.

Months passed, and although people had forgotten about the elephant, the elephant had not forgotten people. She was terrified of being caught again. When the long, lush meadow grass rustled in the night wind, she would startle from her sleep and stampede through the trees, bellowing in fright. Up mountainsides she clambered, down valleys she ran and ran, never at peace. In constant dread, she lived as though she were still tied to her old training post. And in time the great elephant grew deathly thin and weak from exhaustion.

Now in these same mountains lived the Buddha as a Tree-Sprite. Many times he had watched the agitated elephant pace back and forth, back and forth beneath his tree. But now he saw that the elephant would die without some help. Luckily, his chance came soon. It was a scorching summer afternoon, and the great elephant needed relief and rest in the tree's shade, directly below him. The little Sprite quietly slipped into the lowest fork of the tree, appearing very much like leaf-dappled sunshine. Before the elephant had noticed him, and before she could run away in alarm, the Sprite whispered in her ear:

Do you fear the wind
That only blows the leaves away?
So much fear held in your heart
Will waste thee all away!

The elephant heard the Sprite's quiet words and found them soothing. It was a new feeling. She didn't run. Looking up at the tiny Sprite among the leaves, the great elephant wondered if she *did* have anything to be afraid of anymore. After all, here was the smallest creature of the forest telling the biggest not to be afraid! Could it be that she had simply gotten used to being fearful, and maybe, there was a very different way to be?

So, bit by bit the elephant relearned how to enjoy her life in the mountains. Little by little she was able to sleep through the common night sounds of the forest. The dark moonless nights no longer scared her: instead, she beheld a glittering, star-filled sky. She sought out the company of other creatures, frolicked, and played. Thanks to the kindness of the Tree Sprite, the great elephant became strong and healthy and lived very happily, ever after.

And so the Buddha concluded this lesson with the monks. From that day on they treated the restless monk carefully, with kindness and compassion, until finally, his last fear was well gone.

Delight in mindfulness,
Notice your thoughts.

The Monk's Heavy Load

 One fine, warm, spring day, two monks—one young and one old—were traveling to a village far from their monastery to do some trading. In the high mountains where they lived, there were only small trails between villages, no roads and few bridges. This spring had been especially warm. Winter's dense snow was melting quickly and many streams had become too swollen and dangerous to cross.

After walking a distance on a rugged, steep trail, the two monks came upon a fast moving stream where a small, young woman stood timidly on the bank, afraid to cross. The young monk reminded himself that as part of his religious training, he had vowed never to touch anyone of the opposite sex. He nodded to the young woman as he passed her by, lifted his monk's robe up slightly and carefully began to negotiate the stream. But to his amazement, the elder monk sped right past him while carrying the young woman in his arms! When the old monk put her down on the far shore, she bowed respectfully to him in thanks. Not saying a word in reply, he gave her a bright, broad smile and went on his way with a quick step.

The young monk saw that the elder had continued on without him. With some effort he finally managed to catch up. But as they walked on, he considered and considered and reconsidered the old monk's action back at the stream. With each passing mile his thoughts grew angrier and angrier until, hours later, he stopped in his tracks, flushed with rage. He shouted and sputtered at the old monk, "You broke your sacred vows! You were never to touch a woman! How can you forgive yourself? You should not be allowed back to our monastery!"

Surprised at this outburst, the old monk turned to face him. "I dropped that woman hours ago," he said. "Have you been carrying her all this time?"

Getting or losing: how to tell which is which?
I lean here smiling softly to the breeze.
The spider so pleased with his artful web
Has netted only fallen petals,
Not a single bug to eat.

When the Horse Runs Off

 Long ago, in a country where the mountains are among the world's loftiest, there lived an old farmer and his son. The boy spent his days attending to the work of the farm and their one horse—a beautiful white stallion. After years of careful training, the horse ran swifter and smoother than any other in the region. But one day, father and son awoke to find their cherished animal missing.

The son was heartbroken. Neighbors gathered round the two and lamented their great loss. But the father gazed calmly past the villagers to the surrounding high peaks. "We shall see," he said. "We shall see if this is good or if this is bad."

After a week, the magnificent horse returned, followed by an equally fine, wild mare. Father and son soon tamed the new animal. This time, the neighbors praised the old man's remarkable luck—he was now the wealthiest man in town! He owned the two very best horses! But the farmer simply smiled and remarked, "Oh, of course I am pleased . . . but who knows if this is lucky or unlucky?"

And so it came to pass that one day, while racing their splendid horses across the

field, the son fell off and broke both legs badly. While the boy's wounds were cleaned and splinted by the doctor, the villagers bemoaned the family's terrible misfortune. But the father, calm as ever, took comfort in his boy. "He is alive; that is all that counts," replied the old man. "His legs will heal in time. I cannot know if these injuries will turn out to be something good or something bad."

The very next week, a battalion of soldiers marched into the village. A war to the north was underway, and all young men of fighting age were needed immediately. Mothers and fathers gathered food and warm clothing for their boys. With sorrowful good-byes they reluctantly let their sons join the soldiers.

But alas, there was one boy in the village left behind in his bed—for it was obvious his wounds would take many months to heal. The neighbors envied the farmer's good fortune! Of all the young men in town, his son was the only one not taken to war! The old farmer looked out across his fields at the two fine horses grazing. He looked at the lovely way the sun caught the tops of the jagged peaks in the distance, smiled, and said nothing at all.

Let one's boundless love
Fill the whole world—
Above, below and across.

The Noble Ibex: A Jataka Tale

Once upon a time, the Buddha was born as a magnificent ibex. The forest in which he lived was far from civilization and therefore tranquil, inhabited by many creatures both small and large. Its lakes were pristine. Along the banks of clear, babbling brooks were found rare flowers, which blossomed nowhere else on earth. Trees towered above the lush undergrowth and kept the forest cool and mild.

The noble ibex that lived in this forest, the Former Buddha, was as beautiful as he was sleek and swift. He had the body of an animal but the intelligence and empathy of a human being. So deep was his compassion for all living creatures that he often trod delicately so as not to crush anything. He ate nothing but the tips of grasses already gone to seed.

As this region was renowned for its great beauty, hunting parties would at times make long journeys to reach it. On one such occasion, a king and his royal retinue camped on the edge of the forest, hoping to bag large amounts of game before the end of their stay. One morning, the king set out on horseback with his small group following him. Not long after, the king caught glimpse of the splendid ibex and wanted to hunt him down. Snapping his reins across his horse's neck, the king dashed away in chase, leaving the group far behind.

When the ibex heard the quick pounding of hooves, he turned and saw the king swiftly bearing down upon him. The king's bow was drawn taut and an arrow ready in the sites. Although the ibex could have fought the king's attack, he chose to avoid violence, even in self-defense. So the ibex spun around and took off with great speed towards the dense center of the forest, confident the king could not overtake him. Through the thick forest he sprang, still pursued by the king, but the distance between them was increasing. The ibex came to a familiar, small, deep chasm and leapt over it effortlessly. But the king's horse, coming to that same rocky cliff, abruptly pressed his weight backwards and refused to jump. The king had been watching the ibex, not the forest floor. So when the horse stopped with a jolt, the surprised king fell forward, headlong, into the chasm.

After a time, the ibex heard no hoof beats in pursuit. He slowed and twisted his head around to examine the situation behind him. There in the distance he spotted the riderless horse at the chasm's edge and correctly guessed what had happened to the king. A sudden welling of compassion overcame him for his would-have-been murderer. He anticipated that the king must be in severe pain, surely having broken a number of bones in the fall. He knew also that the king would never survive long in this forest: it was rife with tigers and other beasts.

The ibex walked up to the chasm edge and beheld the king far below, moaning and writhing in pain. He no longer looked upon the king as his enemy, but felt his suffering keenly. The Former Buddha gently inquired, "I hope your majesty has no serious wounds? Might the pain of your injuries be diminishing by now?"

The king looked up at the ibex in utter astonishment. He felt a dreadful pang of remorse for his behavior towards this noble animal. Oh, how the king felt his shame!

"You see, your Excellency," comforted the Ibex, " I am no wild devil to be hunted for sport. I am just a peaceful creature living within the bounds of this beautiful forest."

"Oh!" blurted the king. "It is I who acted as a beast, not you! Can you ever forgive me?" he asked. "My physical pain right now," continued the king, "is far less than the pain I feel for having threatened a noble creature as yourself."

"Sire," responded the ibex, "let me help you out of your predicament. I can rescue you if you'll trust me." The ibex took the king's silence as a sign of goodwill and knew that the king would accept his help. He then searched for a boulder as heavy as a man and practiced lifting it. When he felt he could do it safely, without slipping, he made his way down the scree beside the king. "If you mount me as you would your horse, your Excellency, I believe I can leap out of the chasm with you on my back," offered the ibex.

The king followed these directions and held on as best he could. In an instant the ibex leapt in a great arc onto the cliff rim. There the king found his waiting horse but was so overtaken by the goodness of the ibex he could not leave. "What can I do to repay you?" begged the king. "If you would come to my palace, we would see that your every need was met. I can't bear to think of you left in this forest with hunters in pursuit. Please, please come back with me," insisted the king.

"Sire, do you think I, who am so contented in the forest, could really adjust to that? I love nothing better than to live here, in peace. But there is one great favor I would ask of you."

"Anything," said the king.

"I ask that you give up hunting for sport. You now realize that all creatures want happiness and security. Can it be right to do to them what you yourself would despise?

A true king," proclaimed the ibex, "will gain his people's love by showing great goodness, not by showing power."

The grateful king agreed to the request. "Now, let me show you the way back to safety," suggested the ibex. "Mount your horse and I will guide you home to your camp."

The king soon returned to his palace, and the ibex disappeared into the shelter of the forest. But forevermore, the king lived by the wise words of the noble ibex, the Former Buddha. He forbade hunting for sport throughout his kingdom's domain. He protected his people, but no longer waged costly wars against nearby countries. His kingdom flourished. And thus, the good king was greatly loved and respected by his people as the gentlest and wisest of all kings.

Whatever harm an enemy may do to you,
Your own thoughts,
Stormy and uncontrolled,
Will harm you more.

Heaven and Hell

 Long ago in Japan, a samurai—a warrior of those ancient times— went to visit a monk named Hakuin. The samurai was elaborately dressed in armor, and by his side swung a gleaming, sharp sword. He was a big, proud fellow, used to getting whatever he wanted.

"Hakuin!" The samurai bellowed at the temple door, "I want to have a word with you right now!"

Unruffled, the monk ended his meditation with a slow bow. He rose from his meditation bench and took some time to stretch his legs before turning towards his visitor. The large figure of the impatient samurai blocked the temple entrance.

"Well monk," grunted the samurai, "if you know so much and are so wise, tell me all you know about heaven and hell!"

Hakuin inspected the fierce-looking samurai closely. Finally he replied, "You disrupted my meditation to ask something every fool knows? What kind of second-rate soldier are you? You look like a tramp in that outfit! Did you steal that sword from a child? It wouldn't slice a cucumber! Leave this temple and never bother me again!"

If you can picture the reddest plum you've ever seen in your life, you can picture the color of the insulted samurai's face. He was furious! No one ever dared to speak to a samurai rudely—they would surely lose their life before they had time to apologize! In a flash the samurai unsheathed his sword and raised it high over Hakuin's head. "You will *die* for those words little monk!" he roared.

Hakuin looked directly at the warrior. "*This* is what hell feels like," said the monk calmly. The samurai froze, his sword poised in mid-air. In an instant he understood that his anger *did* feel like fire—the fires of a terrible place! The samurai slowly lowered his sword to his side and re-sheathed it. By the time his gaze met the monk's, his anger had vanished as quickly as it had appeared. He felt as if cool water had extinguished the fire: he was grateful and calm.

"And *this* is what heaven feels like," said Hakuin, looking at the samurai's peaceful face.

If you wish to know the truth,
Hold no opinions.

Many Elephants

 Long ago, the Buddha and his followers lived in a park near a city—a place called Jetavana—in a peaceful grove of trees. Many wandering holy men also lived there. Some of the men believed that they alone understood life's secrets. Other holy men had beliefs about life that were just the opposite. And so, the groups argued day and night. "This alone is true! What you think is a flat-out lie!" they shouted.

"How can you be so dense?" another would respond. "How could anyone believe the things you do?"

Finally one morning, after yet another quarrel broke out, a group approached the Buddha and told him about the continuous bickering. When the Buddha heard their story, he gathered all the groups around and told this parable.

Once upon a time, in this very city, the king had a theory he wanted to test. Without revealing his secret, the king ordered his attendants to bring together all the men in the city who had been blind from birth.

"Right away your majesty!" they said and rushed off to do the king's bidding. It was a challenging task to find every last man in the city, but finally the servants accomplished it.

"Your majesty," the head servant announced, "all the men in our city, blind from the time of their birth, are now assembled and waiting for you within the palace courtyard."

"Very well done!" praised the king. And knowing that these men had never seen nor touched an elephant, the king then requested that his gentlest elephant be led to the middle of the courtyard. The great elephant was brought out and stood calmly before them. The king had the men form a great circle around her. "Now, all of you," ordered the king, "slowly reach forward and feel what an elephant is like!"

Some of the blind men touched only the animal's face, while others felt the elephant's giant ears. Some of the men felt the hard tusks. Some touched only the trunk, and some only the belly. Many of the men felt just a leg, and a few just the tail. And to each group the king and his attendants proclaimed the same thing, "*This* is what an elephant is like!"

After a while the king stopped the men and asked, "Have you all felt the elephant? Are each of you very sure what an elephant is like now?"

"Yes, we certainly are!" they shouted.

So the king had the elephant led away. Then he asked, "Tell me, each of you, what exactly is an elephant like?"

The blind man who had felt the animal's head said: "Oh, your majesty, an elephant is like a huge water-pot."

Whereas the man who had touched the ears said: "Your majesty, an elephant feels just like a royal fan."

"Your majesty, an elephant is like a strong plow," said one who had felt the tusks.

And the blind man who had felt only the belly recalled: "An elephant is like a grain bin full of wheat."

The ones who had felt the elephant's tail said, "Well, actually, your majesty, an elephant is much like a giant snake!"

But when all the men heard the different responses, they thought surely the others were lying to their king! Right away an argument broke out among them, and of course none believed any of the others! In no time at all they resorted to shouts and punches. "An elephant feels like a water-pot!"

"It does not! It's like a great plow! I felt it with my own hands!"

"It's not anything like a plow. It's exactly like a giant fan—two of us thought so!"

"An elephant is nothing like what you said!"

"And the king," concluded the Buddha, "was delighted with his experiment! It is precisely like this, O brothers, that you also find so many things to argue about."

Really think about your work—
And search for happiness.
And then?
Do all you can
For those who haven't what you have.

The Worth of Cherry Blossoms

In Japan two centuries ago, there lived a Buddhist nun named Rengetsu. Her life as a nun began tragically, after her husband and young children died. To support herself, she worked as a potter, a poet, and an artist. Her exquisite poetry gained her instant fame. She soon found herself moving from one home to the next, trying to avoid the constant press of customers.

Although Japan named her a Patron Saint of the Arts, she never held on to the money her art brought in—she gave it to those who needed it most. More than a few times she parted with her warm kimono to a shivering street beggar. When a robber entered her home during the night, she lit a lamp for him to see by, then fixed the thief a cup of hot tea while inviting him to discuss his desperate situation.

Rengetsu said she moved about like "a drifting cloud blown by a fierce wind." Her poems are fresh with images from journeys through forests and mountains. On one such pilgrimage to a remote region, she had hiked since noon without having passed through a single village. But at last, as dusk descended, she came upon a small settle-

ment along a riverbank. She knocked upon the door of an inn, humbly asking for a night's lodging. But the inn was already full.

As she rested, stars appeared out of the advancing darkness. The village grew steadily more quiet. The sounds of families enjoying their suppers faded into those of preparing for the night. Rengetsu was tired, but not discouraged. Beyond the town she had earlier spied a forgotten orchard with lush, soft grass beneath the trees. She retraced her steps down the road and bedded down for the night under a cherry tree.

In the middle of the night, she sensed a bright light upon her face. It awakened her. When her eyes opened, a hazy, snowy moon loomed in the cloudless sky. Directly above her, thousands of cherry blossoms had opened while she slept, and each flower now held bright moonlight in its petal cup. It was so lovely Rengetsu gasped. She bowed towards the village, giving thanks for this unexpected gift: a gift of nature far more meaningful than a comfortable night in a bed! Rengetsu then composed this poem:

Through their
Kindness in refusing
Me lodging,

I found myself
Beneath the
Beautiful blossoms

On the night of the
Misty moon.

Thus shall you think
Of all this fleeting world:
A star at dawn, a bubble in a stream,
A flash of lightning in a summer cloud,
A flickering lamp, an illusion, a dream.

The Span of Life

 The Buddha once asked a student, "How long is a human life?"

The student replied, "It is so brief it seems but a day long."

He then asked another the same question, "What is the true length of a person's life?"

She answered thoughtfully, "It is the time taken to eat a single meal."

And so the Buddha asked a third student, "How long is life?"

"The time in a single breath," was the student's reply.

"Exactly so." said the Buddha, "You understand."

When there is anger, offer loving kindness.
When there is selfishness, offer generosity.
When there is deceit, offer the truth.

Teaching a Thief

Bankei was a famous Zen teacher in Japan long ago. Students from all over came to his monastery for months of study and meditation. To make it through such intensive training is not an easy thing: there is much hard work to be done, many hours of meditation, little sleep, and only small, spare meals.

Once, during a time at the monastery, a student found that all he could meditate upon was his empty stomach. It was also all that he thought about during work and all he thought of even when eating! Finally, he could stand it not a day longer. In the night, ever so quietly, he sneaked into the kitchen, hoping to make off with a little something tasty and filling. But the head cook—always alert even when asleep—awoke and caught him.

The next morning, the matter was brought to Bankei in hopes that the student would be forced to leave. However, much to the group's dismay, Bankei thanked them for the information and acted as if nothing had happened.

Just a few days later, the same pupil was caught stealing food from the kitchen again.

The students were even angrier. It was the middle of the night when the thief was apprehended, but they wrote a petition right there and then to their teacher Bankei. They each vowed to leave the monastery the next day if the thief was not expelled.

When Bankei read the petition the next morning, he sighed. He went outside to the monastery gardens and paced thoughtfully. At last he asked that all the monks and students—including the thief—be brought together. They gathered in the temple hall, becoming quiet when Bankei entered.

"Many of you have come from far away to be here," announced Bankei. "Your hard work and perseverance are to be praised. You are excellent, dedicated students. You have also clearly shown me that you know right from wrong. If you wish, you may leave this monastery and find another teacher. But I must tell you that the thief will remain, even as my only student."

The students were appalled! A murmur of discontent hummed about the room. How could their teacher ask *them* to leave? *Who* had done the wrong thing? Only the thief! Feeling the anger of the other students, the thief in their midst hung his head in disgrace.

"My friends," Bankei gently continued, "this thief does not understand the difference between right and wrong as you do. If he leaves, how will these things be learned? He needs to stay here so he can also understand."

When the thief heard these words, he felt profoundly moved. Tears sprung to his eyes. But even through his shame in front of the others, he felt Bankei's deep compassion. He knew he would not steal anymore.

Bankei ended his speech. He left the hall, leaving the students to make their individual decisions. The thief immediately took a spot on a meditation bench and set about meditating. Many of the students stood right up to leave the monastery. Somewhat confused by Bankei's speech, they discussed things among themselves. All except for the presence of one student—the thief—the great hall emptied for a time.

When Bankei returned an hour later, it was so very quiet he assumed all the students had left, just as they had vowed. But much to his surprise, every last student had returned. All were quietly sitting, composed in meditation. The wise and kind Bankei smiled at such a wonderful sight.

Those who remain tranquil
When feeling another's anger,
Protect themselves
And all other beings.

Anger

One day, the Buddha and a large following of monks and nuns were passing through a village. The Buddha chose a large shade tree to sit beneath so the group could rest awhile out of the heat. He often chose times like these to teach, and so he began to speak. Soon, villagers heard about the visiting teacher and many gathered around to hear him.

One surly young man stood to the side, watching as the crowd grew larger and larger. To him, it seemed that there were too many people traveling from the city to his village, and each had something to sell or teach. Impatient with the bulging crowd of monks and villagers, he shouted at the Buddha, "Go away! You just want to take advantage of us! You teachers come here to say a few pretty words and then ask for food and money!"

But the Buddha was unruffled by these insults. He remained calm, exuding a feeling of loving-kindness. He politely requested that the man come forward. Then he asked, "Young sir, if you purchased a lovely gift for someone, but that person did not accept the gift, to whom does the gift then belong?"

The odd question took the young man by surprise. "I guess the gift would still be mine because I was the one who bought it."

"Exactly so," replied the Buddha. "Now, you have just cursed me and been angry with me. But if I do not accept your curses, if I do not get insulted and angry in return, these curses will fall back upon you—the same as the gift returning to its owner."

The young man clasped his hands together and slowly bowed to the Buddha. It was an acknowledgment that a valuable lesson had been learned. And so the Buddha concluded for all to hear, "As a mirror reflects an object, as a still lake reflects the sky: take care that what you speak or act is for good. For goodness will always cast back goodness, and harm will always cast back harm."

I want this, I want that!
Is but foolishness.
Here's a secret—
All things are impermanent.

Gifts for the Robber

Ryokan is one of the best-loved poets of ancient Japan. He was also a Buddhist monk. He lived as a hermit—very simply, all alone in a small mountain hut. He wrote short, lovely poems about his lonely life, nature, and the children in the nearby village that he loved to play with. A begging bowl, a monk's robe, and a book or two were all he owned.

One afternoon, when Ryokan was away in the village, a thief arrived at his hut. But much to his dismay, there was truly nothing to steal. As the thief lingered, considering the situation, he didn't hear the returning footsteps of Ryokan. When the door suddenly opened, the thief's surprised and guilty expression told Ryokan the whole story. Nevertheless, the monk warmly welcomed him. "Oh Sir!" Ryokan bellowed cheerily. "What kindness! You have traveled a great distance to visit me!" He grabbed the man's hand and shook it enthusiastically. "I could never allow you to leave without some show of my hospitality! I must find a proper gift for you!"

But they both looked around the bare hut and knew there was no gift to give. The

thief awkwardly backed up towards the door, trying to take his leave. But Ryokan brightened with an idea. He began to disrobe quickly. "Ah! I have it! Don't go yet. Here is something for all your trouble," the monk suggested. "Please, take my clothes! I apologize for such a meager gift. It seems to be all that I can offer right now."

The thief, feeling very sheepish indeed, could do nothing but accept the clothes Ryokan placed in his arms. Wondering if this monk wasn't truly crazy, the thief reached for the door and quickly escaped into the night. "Be sure to visit again soon!" Ryokan shouted after him.

Then the monk sat down beside his window overlooking the mountains. As the evening sky above darkened to indigo, the east lightened to bronze. Soon a huge, golden moon slipped above the mountain ridge. Ryokan, naked and shivering, sat contentedly. He watched for a long, long while as the spectacular moon ascended the sky.

"Poor man," he mumbled to himself. "I gave him such worthless things! If only I could have given him this wonderful moon." He then wrote his most famous haiku poem:

The thief failed to take it—
The moon shining
At the window.

We must all face death;
Those who really know it
Put aside their quarrels.

The Quarrelsome Quails: A Jataka Tale

 When the Buddha lived in the Kingdom of Kosala, he headed large communities of monks and nuns. Within such big groups, quarrels were inevitable at times. One squabble in particular never seemed to resolve itself. At last the Buddha felt he must address it. He brought the communities together and spoke to them; "Strife between people is ugly and never, ever helpful. In bygone times, animals cooperating with each other defeated their enemies. But as soon as they fought among themselves," the Buddha cautioned, "they perished. Listen to their story from long ago."

Once upon a time, many years ago, the Future Buddha was born as a handsome quail. He lived in a beautiful forest, the king of a thousand quails. The forest was a paradise. The songs of colorful birds wove through the treetops, water gushed from abundant springs, flowers adorned each plant, and ripe fruit could be plucked at every turn.

But one day, a hunter entered the forest in search of quail. He brought a whistle that exactly mimicked the distress call of a quail—the cry of a quail in trouble. Carefully hiding in the bushes, the hunter blew the whistle until a group of quail came eagerly running towards the sound. As the quails looked for their companion, the hunter leapt from the bush, flung his net over the birds, and tightened the side cords. He then stuffed the whole lot into his basket and brought them home to be sold and eaten.

The hunter had been so successful that he came again the next day, and the next. He was able to capture so many birds that he could barely lift his heavy load. But it wasn't long before the king quail, the Future Buddha, took notice that his flock was greatly diminished. He decided some precautions must be taken immediately, before any more lives were lost. He gathered his flock together and warned, "This hunter is making the lives of our families very short and very frightening! Every day, we hear the terrible cries of our brothers and sisters as they are carried off in the hunter's bag! But listen! I have a plan, which will make it impossible for him to catch even one more bird." The king pressed on; "When that hunter throws the net, each of us must quickly find a hole to poke our head through. Then, all together, on the count of three, we must fly away with the entire net to a thorn bush. While the net is caught on the thorns," the king quail proclaimed, "we can escape underneath before the hunter finds us! If we work all together like this, if we cooperate, I know we can escape with our lives." The birds repeated the king's plan back to him, making sure they had it right. Then the quails agreed to try it as soon as the hunter next tricked them.

The following day, they got their chance. Huddled together in a group, they were fooled once more by the hunter's whistle. The dark shadow of the net loomed overhead and then encircled them. But they quickly remembered the king quail's idea. Trying to remain brave, each quail put its head through a hole in the net and counted one, two, and three! Up they flew, all together, lifting the net with them. It seemed a miracle! And as they flew, they searched for the first thorny bush to land upon. There they left the net in tangles on the topmost thorns while they skittered away underneath.

From a safe distance, they watched cheerfully as the hunter disentangled his net from the bush over several hour's time. Finally, the man packed up his belongings. For the first time in many days, he went home with a completely empty basket.

During the weeks that followed, the quails played the same trick on the hunter again and again. They tittered gleefully while watching him untangle the net. But as the days passed and the hunter caught no food, he grew afraid for his family. He would not have enough food or money for the coming winter. When he returned home, his worried wife asked, "What has happened? It's been weeks since you've caught any meat! We will surely starve if this continues!"

"Ah, dear wife," said the hunter reassuringly, "at first I couldn't believe my own eyes, but those quails have learned to cooperate with each other! They foil my best plans! The moment my net lands upon them, they fly off as one bird! I have to search for my net that they have hidden in the woods. When I find it, it lies tangled in a hundred knots upon a bush!" The wife looked at him anxiously. "But have no fear my dearest," chuckled the hunter, "they can't continue to work together like this for much longer. Mark my words, they will start bickering among themselves soon and we shall bag the whole flock! We shall have full stomachs again in no time, I promise you!"

And so it soon came to pass, just as the hunter had predicted. The quails began to bicker. It seemed to start innocently enough. One of the quails, aiming to land on the feeding grounds, landed instead upon another bird's head. "Hey!" shouted the startled quail, "do you need flying lessons?"

"It was just an accident, I promise!" stammered the clumsy bird.

"Sure!" rebuked the first quail, "Don't you have two eyes?"

Another bird chimed in, "Well, I saw him land and I don't think it was any accident!"

And yet another quail standing nearby remarked, "I watched it too, and you're a worm-head if you think that happened on purpose!"

"Oh yeah?" retorted the bird.

"Yeah!" shouted the other. "And I bet you're such a feather-brain you believe that you alone lift the hunter's net when we escape!"

"Well," boasted the quail, "as a matter of fact I *do* think I am stronger than the rest of you! In fact, I probably *do* lift more than my share!"

And so it went on and on without going anywhere—as all arguments are wont to do. The group quarreled so loudly that the Future Buddha, the king quail, couldn't help but hear them from a distance in the forest. He flew to them and said, "Remember I have cautioned you! There's no peace or safety with anyone who quarrels. Stop now, or I fear you will all die when the hunter comes next!"

But as soon as the king quail left, an angry quail whispered yet a last insult to the quail he'd argued with, giving him a sharp peck to boot. And just as before, a number of quails took sides with one or another of the birds.

When the king quail heard them arguing again so soon, he knew he could do nothing more to stop it. So off he flew to a peaceful feeding ground with the birds that chose not to bicker.

Shortly, the hunter returned to the forest to try his luck again. As always, he lured the birds together by imitating the song of a quail in distress. He flung his net over them. One by one they poked their heads through the net holes. But before counting to three, a still sore quail said, "They say when *you* lift the net, the feathers of your head get mussed and so you just give up! You've never done your share! I'm not moving until you go first! Go ahead, lift away!"

The other quail rejoined, "Someone told me that when *you* lift the net you just tag along. Now's *your* turn. *You* go first!" And so while they each demanded the other to lift, the hunter himself lifted the net. He stuffed the whole lot into his basket and carried them off.

The quails which stayed with the Future Buddha heard the sad cries of the captured birds. They knew it was too late to save them. Then and there they made a vow always to cooperate. They worked hard at their promise and fooled the hunter the rest of their days and lived happily, ever after.

"Thus," said the Buddha, ending his lesson, "No good can ever come from quarrelling—only harm and sometimes, even death." The Buddha, his monks and nuns, then sat in silence and thought deeply and long upon these things.

The beauty of the mountain colors;
What could it have to do
With being right or wrong?

Two Teachers and Tea

 About a century ago in Japan, there lived a Zen teacher named Nan-in. One day, a university professor came to call on Nan-in at his temple.

"Come in, come in for some tea!" welcomed the old Zen master, leading the professor into the tearoom. They sat down across from each other at a small, bare table. The old master sat in silence, perfectly at ease. Occasionally he smiled at the professor warmly; other times he gazed out the window at the enchanting temple gardens.

But the professor grew increasingly edgy with the silence. He squirmed. He tapped his fingers on the table mindlessly. He fixed his eyes anxiously upon the door through which the tea should have arrived. Finally, the professor couldn't bear the silence a minute longer. The only thing that came to his mind to discuss was a lecture on Buddhism he'd just given at the university. And so, clearing his throat loudly, the professor began a lengthy speech.

The old master, Nan-in, made a fine audience. He nodded in a friendly way at the professor's most outstanding points and seemed to have a look of unending curiosity. So the professor was encouraged to keep going—after all, lecturing was his business.

After a half-hour, still no tea had arrived, but the professor thought it might be impolite to bring attention to that fact. He continued with his speech on Buddhism; Nan-in continued to be the most courteous of audiences.

At last, an attendant carried in an elegant tray with a ceremonial teapot and two cups for the men. Nan-in smiled in his relaxed way. In the deliberate manner of a Japanese tea ceremony, he carefully placed a teacup before his chattering guest. Then Nan-in slowly began to pour the hot liquid into his guest's cup. He poured, and continued to pour, until tea water ran like a small waterfall over the cup's brim and into his guest's lap. At this point, the professor's lecture came to an abrupt halt.

"What are you doing?" he sputtered at Nan-in. "Can't you see that there's no more room in this cup?"

Nan-in looked at his visitor earnestly, "Just like this cup, sir, you are also too full. You have too many ideas and opinions to learn. Please first empty your own cup, then together we can learn something useful about Buddhism."

To be firmly attached to an opinion
Or to look down upon other's opinions
Are barriers to true wisdom.

The Buddha and the Brahmins

 Long ago, a number of Brahmins paid a visit to the Buddha. Brahmins were the wealthiest and best-educated religious group in India. On this occasion, they hoped to discuss questions of philosophy with the Buddha. One among them, sixteen-year-old Kapathika, was an exceptional scholar. He wanted to pose the very first question.

"Venerable Buddha," Kapathika asked, "we study the Holy Scriptures of the Brahmins. These scriptures are just the same as our fathers studied, and their great-great grandfathers before them. As far back in time as we have been Brahmins, these have been our holy teachings. We've come to the firm conclusion that our teachings alone are true. Therefore, it follows that everything taught by others is false. Now, sir, what is your opinion about this?"

The Buddha considered the question in silence. After a time, he posed a question back to the Kapathika: "Young sir, among all the Brahmins, is there any one person who will guarantee that in all the world over, from the beginning of time and forever more, your teachings alone are true, and all others false?'"

The young man hesitated. "No," he finally replied, " I've never heard anyone guarantee such a claim."

"Then," continued the Buddha, "is there a teacher, or a teacher of teachers, or any author of your scriptures, who knows and guarantees: 'The Brahmin teachings alone are true, and everything else in the world is false?'"

"No, I don't believe so," answered the young man truthfully.

"Then it seems to me that the claim of the Brahmins is like a long line of blind men, each holding the hand of the next one in front. The first fellow can't clearly see his destination, nor can the middle one, nor can the last. Yet they won't let go of one another; they remain a group." The Buddha pressed on, "Young Kapathika, a wise man or woman can say, 'I have a faith,' or 'I believe in this.' To say so is respectful of truth. But a wise man and wise woman will never claim: 'This alone, in all the world over, is true, and everything else is false.'"

And with those thoughtful words, by which all opinions are respected, the Buddha, young Kapathika, and the Brahmins were able to continue discussing many vital things late into the night.

A broad heart can encompass
Every imaginable thing.

The Broom Master

Long ago, during the time of the Buddha, lived a boy named Chundaka. Chunda—as he was fondly called—was a happy and good youngster, but unable to learn to read or write. In comparison, Chunda's older brother became quite knowledgeable, with a keen interest in Buddhism. When the older brother decided to lead a monk's life, Chunda followed along. He sought to live near his brother, but secretly, he also hoped to work alongside the monks and learn about Buddhism.

"Why don't you ask the Buddha if you can become a monk, too?" his brother encouraged. But Chunda had no confidence.

"Brother, how can I?" Chunda sadly replied. "I can't memorize, and I can't read or write. I have no knowledge of scriptures, and I won't be able to learn them. A monk must be able to teach others many things."

But his brother assured him that both riches and knowledge were meaningless to the Buddha. "He values only the compassion we have for one another and the ways to help all creatures suffer less. No one is as gentle and kind as he is. I know he will not disappoint you, Chunda. Go and hear for yourself," prodded his brother hopefully.

So Chunda mustered all his courage. He bathed and purified himself. When he was certain he was quite ready, he approached the Buddha. The Buddha observed that this humble young man had an earnest and pure heart. He could see that Chunda would try his very best. The Buddha welcomed him as the newest monk in the community.

The next morning, Ananda, head of all the monks, gave Chunda a small scripture to memorize, just 6 lines long. It was the first of hundreds that each monk was expected to learn by heart. But a week later, having tried his hardest, poor Chunda could still not recite it from beginning to end. Completely disheartened, he went back to the Buddha and admitted his failure.

But the Buddha was not greatly disappointed; he had total faith in Chunda's good intentions. The Buddha and Chunda sat thoughtfully together in silence. An idea suddenly occurred to the Buddha. "Chunda, are you a hard worker?" asked the Buddha. "Do you think you can sweep the temple and keep it spotlessly clean?"

"Oh yes, teacher. I'm a good worker, and I'm very good at sweeping. I just cannot seem to learn scripture."

So the Buddha gave Chunda the task of keeping the temple perfectly clean. He was to hold no other job but temple sweeper. The Buddha then requested that Chunda speak two lines while sweeping: *remove all dust, remove all dirt.*

But as soon as poor Chunda attempted his task, the words completely vanished from his mind. Luckily, Ananda overheard the Buddha's instructions and could help Chunda remember them over and over again.

At last, a month later, Chunda had it learned by heart. "Remove all dust," the monks heard Chunda whisper with the sweep of the broom. "Remove all dirt," he murmured with the return sweep.

Behind Chunda's back, the other monks snickered at his memory problem. More than a few took some pride in the extent of their learning. Day and night Chunda poured his heart into his work, repeating those six words again and again. Eventually, however, over time every monk couldn't help but admire Chunda's perseverance. They had never witnessed such single-minded determination.

In time, the few words that the Buddha had given him to memorize became more and more meaningful to Chunda. His chores became a meditation upon the words. Chunda's curiosity deepened, and he suspected that the Buddha knew all along that these words were not as simple as they first appeared. "Did my teacher want me to sweep *outer* dust and dirt or *inner* dust and dirt?" he wondered. "What *is* inner dirt? How would one go about *cleaning* inner dirt?" he asked himself many times.

Some months later, Chunda found the answers to these questions himself. While he worked, insight nudged its way into his heart. Once in awhile now, the monks saw Chunda thoughtfully pausing from his endless task, leaning against his broom and looking at the far off horizon.

At last a day came when Chunda felt ready to discuss his thoughts with the Buddha. "Venerable sir," said Chundaka enthusiastically, "I think I finally understand the real meaning of the words you gave me."

"Please tell me what you understand," encouraged the Buddha.

"I believe that inner dust and dirt is a grasping," said Chunda. "If we don't like something in our lives, we grasp for a different situation. But if we really like something that we have, then we also grasp because we don't want it to change." Chunda continued, "To look at life clearly, we must always see through this. We must sweep the dust and dirt away and keep our inner temple clean." The Buddha smiled warmly at Chunda's thoughtful words.

And so, as the years passed, Chunda swept and meditated and thought deeply. He found he did not have to memorize scriptures as the other monks did, for teachings seemed to arise from within. After a time, he became known as one of the wise and gentle teachers of Buddhism, affectionately called "Chundaka, the Broom Master." He lived a long and happy life. And for many years people journeyed to the monastery from distant places, not just to hear from the learned monks, but to listen especially to Chundaka, the Broom Master. He was their favorite, loved for his very simple, yet very wise sayings.

Purify your heart;
There is no place to hide.

The Old Teacher's Test: A Jataka Tale

Once, while the Buddha slept, an argument broke out in the middle of the night between his fivehundred monks. Although they tried to keep quiet, the Buddha heard them and awoke. In the middle of the night he gathered the entire group together and spoke to them. "My friends, in olden times, the wise ones believed that a bad deed could never be hidden; a crime can never be a secret for long," said the Buddha. "Therefore, a wise person never gives in to wrongdoing. Monks, listen to this story I will tell you from years past."

Long ago, an old, wise teacher decided to put his students to a test. "My dear pupils," he announced, "you have been loyal and so hard working! We have studied and learned things of great importance from ancient, noble teachings. But alas," he continued, "your teacher has now grown quite old. Have you noticed how white my hair has turned? How my painful, old bones cause me to lumber like a turtle?"

"Yes, we have noticed these things, teacher," said a boy, and the group nodded in silent agreement.

"Well," said the old teacher, "I'm afraid I can no longer support this school. It now falls upon each of you to find the money to keep the school open."

"Of course!" the group cried. "We will do whatever we can!"

"But sir," paused a boy, "how would we do it? We only know how to perform our family chores! We have no means to earn money yet." Troubled voices rippled across the room.

"Children, children," quieted the old teacher, "know that gold and riches are everywhere! If you look carefully, you will see that people have many more things than they need. It wouldn't hurt them even a little to share some of it with us!" The students looked nervously at one another, wondering if the words they were hearing from their teacher could be sincere.

"So here's what I want you to do," the wise, old teacher pushed on. "Journey to the city today and find a quiet alley between the main streets. Sooner or later, a wealthy man or woman, adorned in gold and wearing robes of finest silk, will come along. In the blink of an eye, you must take their purse without anyone watching. If no one has seen you, I will accept what you bring and then we will sell it. But if you allow yourselves to be seen, I will refuse any item, even if it be diamonds and rubies!"

The students were astonished and pained by their teacher's bold request. They fixed their gaze upon the floor and avoided each other's eyes. "Remember," the teacher said, trying to convince them, "I would never ask you to do what I myself wouldn't do. I have never lied to you. Surely our school will put the money to better uses than the rich people do!"

"Well then," a student humbly replied, "we will do what you ask of us, teacher."

"Then now is the time to go," said the old teacher, ushering them out the door. "Go quickly and return soon! You will find it very easy when no one is watching."

And so saying, the students filed out the door, setting off towards the city. The group buzzed with a mix of fear and excitement. But when the room emptied, there, in silence, stood a lone boy.

The teacher noticed and gently approached him. "What is the matter? All my other students are brave and willing to help their poor, old teacher. Why aren't you going along with them?"

With a head shyly bent forward, the boy whispered, "Master, I cannot do what you have asked me to do!"

"Oh? And why is that?"

"Because," answered the boy, "there is no place on earth where no one watches. There is no such secret place. Even if I'm all by myself, I will see myself steal!"

At this response the old teacher hugged the boy joyfully. "At least one of my students understood my true meaning! You were the only one who really listened. I am very proud of you!" he exclaimed.

The boy smiled warmly in return, "Thank you, teacher."

And when the rest of the students came back for the missing boy, they saw that their teacher had meant his request as a test, and they felt deeply ashamed. But from that day forward, they never forgot the brave boy's words, "Wherever I am, someone always watches." And they all lived by this guide and grew up to be wise, good, and honest people.

The Buddha then ended his solemn lesson with the monks, saying that he himself had been the young student years ago.

For never in this world
Do hatreds cease through hatred;
Through love alone do they end.
This is the ancient and eternal law.

Prince Dighavu

Once, some monks who could not stop quarreling came to the Buddha to ask his advice. "Brothers," the Buddha calmly replied, "I have told you many times that fights and quarrels solve no problems—yet you continue. Remember, even some kings with great and powerful armies have learned gentleness. So much the more that you, living the holy life without possessions, should be like light in the world, known far and wide for kindness. Listen now to this story of a noble prince, who became a true hero in the world."

Once upon a time, two kingdoms lay side by side. One kingdom belonged to the King of Kasi: a powerful ruler who possessed a great army and treasuries bursting with gold. But in the nearby kingdom of Kosala lived a much poorer king. He led a meager army, possessed little gold, and held sway over a modest territory. And just as you might guess, the powerful King of Kasi eyed the small kingdom of Kosala and decided he should conquer it.

When the King of Kosala heard that a large garrison was headed his way, he knew he didn't stand a chance. To avoid any bloodshed, he counseled with his ministers and decided to immediately surrender his army. As the attacking warriors approached, the King of Kosala slipped away to the city's edge—he and the queen disguised as humble potters.

After a time concealed among the common folk, the queen gave birth to a beautiful baby boy. He was secretly named and crowned, Prince Dighavu. They so loved their new son, that the king and queen's only concern became his safety. The king feared that somehow—at some time in the future—the royal family would be recognized. He felt it was only a matter of time; a spy would see through their disguises and kill them all. So with heartfelt loss, the King and Queen of Kosala sent their young prince away to be raised in the countryside.

Alas, a dozen years later, events occurred exactly as the king had feared. The present barber of the King of Kasi had once been the barber to the poorer king. And one day, in the hubbub of the busy marketplace, the barber recognized the disguised king. He easily saw through the king's charade. The barber fell back into the crowd and secretly pursued the king to discover where he now lived. Then the barber reported right away to the King of Kasi, knowing that he would be richly rewarded for the information. "I have news that right within the walls of this city live both the King and Queen of Kosala! I, who know the king's face better than any, saw it with my own eyes—they live in a potter's shed and are disguised as beggars!"

When the King of Kasi heard this report, he feared that if the old king and queen were yet alive, they had a hundred reasons to seek his own death and the return of their kingdom. Disguised or not, he anticipated they would find an opportunity to kill him. So he commanded his guards, "Go now to the potters' sheds near the outskirts of town. Arrest the old king and queen! When you find them, it will be their last hour! Bind their arms, shave their heads, bring them outside the gates of the city and destroy them!" And thus the guards were dispatched to capture the couple.

But very early this same day, the young Prince Dighavu awoke full of longing to be with his parents. Now old enough to travel from village to city alone, he reasoned, "It's been months since I've seen my parents. I would so much like to visit with them today! I will make them a present of ripened fruit and delicious cheese from the country." And so the prince cheerfully gathered a few gifts, packed some clothing and money, and set out for the city.

By this time, however, the guards had found the royal couple—just exactly where the barber had betrayed them to be. They bound their arms tightly with thick rope and dragged them roughly through the streets. But the king and queen walked with dignity, even as they reached the city gates where they knew they would soon die.

And so it came to pass that just as Prince Dhigavu was entering the city, he witnessed his parents being led to their deaths. In desperation, he made his way to the front of the surrounding crowd. Just at the moment he spied his parents, they too, saw him amidst the mob. When the prince neared within earshot, his father shouted, "Dear Dighavu, do not look long! Do not look short! For hatred is not stopped by more hatred! No, dear one, hatred ends only by love!"

The soldiers thought the old king had lost his mind. "Who is this Dhigavu? What gibberish you speak!"

But the king cautioned Dhigavu twice more in the same way, finishing, "He that is intelligent will understand my meaning!" These were the king's last words. As swords fell upon his parents' heads, the anguished prince said a silent farewell so as not to reveal his own identity.

Prince Dhigavu went to the nearby forest and fell to the ground. In agony he wept and wept until he could weep no more. Under the empty night sky, he considered the terrible murder of his parents and devised a plan to recover his family's honor.

First, he returned to the city, and purchased some liquor for the soldiers standing guard over his parents. When the guards succumbed to the alcohol and fell asleep, the prince performed a funeral by the city gates. But at that same, exact moment, from atop the splendid palace tower, the King of Kasi happened to see the prince paying his respects to the murdered king and queen. "Alas!" said the king in great alarm. "What misfortune will happen now? I will still have no safety or peace of mind while someone who cares for them wishes to revenge their deaths!"

And so it came to pass that the very next day Prince Dhigavu embarked on such a plan. He went to the king's elephant stable and asked that the elephant trainer teach him his art. The trainer agreed to take on the eager apprentice. As part of the prince's secret plan, he rose each day at dawn to play the lute and sing to the entire palace compound. His lovely songs were haunting and captivating. Just as the prince had hoped, the King of Kasi, standing on his palace balcony, heard the enchanting voice and asked his attendants from whence it came. "Your Majesty," they replied, "it is the elephant trainer's new apprentice."

"Bring him to me," commanded the king. "I must meet the one who possesses such a gift."

All was proceeding exactly in accord with Prince Dighavu's plan. He came before the king, strummed the lute even more beautifully, and sang his most soothing melodies. The king was utterly charmed. "Young man," said the king, "such a voice comes only from one with the finest sensibilities and depth of feeling. I would like you to have the honor of being my manservant." So Prince Dighavu—still unknown for his real identity—became the king's personal attendant. He rose before the king, preparing the king's affairs; he retired at night long after the king, securing the king's affairs; and he obeyed the king's every command in between. And in due time, the king appointed Prince Dighavu as Councilor and Confidant—just as the prince had hoped.

But Prince Dhigavu's secret and grand scheme was far from complete. A year or so later, the prince had the chance he had worked and waited for. It so happened that one balmy, spring day, the king wished to go for a chariot ride. To Prince Dighavu he requested, "Harness the chariot, my best man; I wish to go hunting in the forest and I want you alone to drive me."

"Yes, your majesty, right away!" obeyed the prince. A magnificent chariot of gold and lapis was harnessed to two steeds. The prince firmly held the reins and hurried the chariot towards the city's perimeter. As the city's gates opened wide for the royal chariot, Prince Dhigavu saw the king's army go in the direction of the eastern forest; the Prince steered the chariot towards the west. "I believe the hunting will be better in these quieter woods sire," he assured the king.

"Very well, my man. Let us try it out," replied the king.

The day was cloudless, and after an hour of travel, the heat oppressive. The sultry, midday sun made the king grow drowsy. "My man, unharness the chariot," he mumbled. "I am tired and I wish to lie down in the shade of some trees."

"Yes, your majesty," complied the prince. The prince watered and hobbled the horses, then rested beside the king under a large Banyan tree. The king placed his trusting head in the prince's lap and fell immediately to sleep.

With the king's safety resting utterly in the hands of Prince Dighavu, the prince's plan was nearly complete. As the prince looked upon the sleeping king, he thought to himself, "The King of Kasi has done me as much harm as any man could. He has murdered my mother and father! He has robbed our kingdom of its treasury and territory! He has destroyed the honor of the Kingdom of Kosala! Now is the time for me to avenge my hatred!"

Ever so quietly, the prince unsheathed his sword. But as he raised his sword over the king, ready to inflict his punishment, his father's last words seemed to shout within him: *Dighavu, hatred is not stopped by more hatred! No, dear one, hatred ends only by love!* Prince Dighavu could not disobey his father's dying words. He could not kill this unsuspecting king. The prince slowly sheathed his sword. But then the same thought of revenge—the thought that had been his mission since the day of his parents' deaths—rose in him more strongly! He had waited years for this moment! Again, he unsheathed his sword. But alas, he stopped himself once more; he could not act against his father's last wish; he could not end his hatred with another murder.

Suddenly, the king awoke and sat bolt upright—pale and terrified! The prince's internal struggle abruptly ended. "Your Majesty!" said the prince, "what ever has occurred? Why did you wake so alarmed?"

The king gasped, "Right now, in my dream, the son of the King of Kosala—the heir and prince—wanted to kill me by sword. He was going to sever my head! I thought I was about to die!"

Then Prince Dighavu, gently touching the neck of the king with his left hand and drawing his sword with the other, told him the truth. "I, your majesty, am that prince! I am Prince Dighavu, son of the King of Kosala! You have robbed my people of food, territory, and treasure. You have even killed my own mother and father! This would indeed be the time to show my hatred and exact my revenge!"

At that admission, the king fell upon his knees at the feet of the prince and begged for forgiveness. "Grant me my life, dear Dighavu! Grant me my life!" wept the king.

In his heart, Prince Dighavu now realized what his father had meant for him to learn. He told the king of his father's forgiving words—his last words—and how they stopped the prince from ending the king's life. The prince proclaimed that he would no longer carry this terrible hatred. "Although I have the power to grant you your life at this moment," said the prince to the king, "you also have the power to grant me my life: for you can assure my safety in your kingdom!"

"This is true," agreed the king. "Grant me my life now and I'll forever grant you yours. We will no longer be enemies, but vow to live in peace." At that, the prince and king swore an oath never to harm one another and to protect each other's well being.

Peaceful now, with a warm feeling of forgiveness, the two men harnessed the horses, remounted the chariot, and leisurely made their way back to the palace. When the king returned to his court, he gathered all his ministers and councilors together. "Tell me sirs," asked the king, "if it happened that you laid eyes upon Prince Dighavu, son of the King of Kosala, what would you do?"

A minister immediately spoke up, "Your majesty, we would kill him on the spot!"

"Yes!" shouted another. "We would chop off his head and cut him to pieces!" Many voices rose in a cacophony of agreement.

But the king said, "Hush! Sirs, in front of you is Prince Dighavu, son of the King of Kosala." A great, astonished silence filled the hall. The king continued, "You may not harm him. He has granted me my life and I have granted him his." The king turned to the prince; "I would like you to tell them, young prince, the marvelous meaning of your father's last words."

All eyes in the court turned to the prince. He looked at his audience with courage and forgiveness. "When my father said to me in his hour of death, 'Look not long dear Dhigavu' what he meant was, 'Do not hold on to hatred, do not nurture it.' When, Your

Majesty, my father spoke, 'Look not short,' what he meant was, 'Do not lose friends easily—be the most loyal of friends.' When my father said, 'Hatred is not stopped by more hatred!' what he wanted me to learn was this: the king has had my mother and father killed. Were I to kill Your Majesty, your people would want to kill me, and my people would want to kill those who had harmed me. Hatred would not end by further hatred. On and on it would go, with many lives lost and many hearts broken. But now," continued the prince, turning towards the king, "Your Majesty has given me my life and safety, and I have done the same for you. So by love and forgiveness we have stopped this terrible cycle of hatred."

The king blessed the prince, "Oh, councilors! Is it not remarkable how deeply the prince understands his father's brief words!" And thus the king returned to Prince Dhigavu the army, territory, and treasure that rightfully belonged to the Kingdom of Kosala. The prince and the king's own daughter were soon married, and they all lived in peace, two kingdoms side by side, happily ever after.

"And so I say to you," declared the Buddha to the monks, "enough of fighting! This is my advice, good brothers." And the Buddha returned to the solace of his meditation.

Although we are here today,
Tomorrow cannot be guaranteed.
Keep this in mind! Keep this in mind!

A Man, Two Tigers, and a Strawberry

Once, a man gathering wood from the forest floor looked up to find himself eye to eye with a ferocious tiger. He chucked his load of wood at the tiger, turned, and fled as quickly as human legs would move. He wove through the forest trees, dodged around boulders, and jumped over thorny bushes with the tiger as close as a shadow behind him. Just as the man felt the tiger's hot breath on his neck and the nick of a sharp claw through his shirt, he came to the edge of a high cliff. Without a thought, the man grabbed a thick vine within reach and slung himself over the cliff face. Letting the vine slide through his hands he quickly lowered out of the tiger's reach. He heard his own heart pounding furiously; he could barely catch a breath, but he felt so relieved to have escaped!

As the man looked around to take stock of his situation, he glanced down at the base of the cliff. There, with a tail snaking leisurely back and forth, sat another tiger— her wide eyes intently fixed upon him as he dangled from above. Just then, the man noticed that the vine he held vibrated ever so slightly. He looked up to see a pair of mice, poised on a mouse-sized ledge, nibbling away at the single vine on which his life hung. His truly desperate situation was dawning upon him, yet something shimmering and red caught his eye and made him investigate. He looked closely and found a luscious, plump strawberry growing right out of a crack in the cliff. With one arm clutching the vine, he reached over with his free arm and plucked it. It was the most delicious morsel he'd ever tasted!

A fool is his own foe.

The Dung Beetle: A Jataka Tale

During the Buddha's lifetime, small groups of monks and nuns stopped in villages with their begging bowls in hand. They had taken vows of poverty and, thus, had to beg for their one meal a day. But in a certain village, a young man was known to follow and taunt the monks as they went from door to door. Finally, one monk grew so frustrated with the boy, he threw some dung at him to make him stop. Later, when the Buddha heard the story, he told the monks and nuns this tale of the past.

In olden times, when it was difficult and sometimes dangerous to travel, a group of merchants had to journey across a wide desert to reach a mountain village on the other side. After many days of hardship, they succeeded in crossing the great desert without losing a person or animal to the heat. In the shade of the hills and trees, they held a feast in celebration. They camped beside a cool river and roasted fresh meat over fires. They drank liquor and danced happily late into the night. Well before the heat of the following day, they had harnessed their horses and set off again to reach the mountain village.

But when the merchants had left, a little dung beetle—no bigger than your eye—smelled the scraps of the feast and scampered along in the direction of the campsite. Although the leftovers would have been mere crumbs to you and I, to the dung beetle they looked like a year's supply of food! Furthermore, everywhere the dung beetle looked, he saw puddles of liquor where the travelers had emptied their bottles. Being that it was now the heat of the day, and being that the little dung beetle was quite thirsty himself, he drank a puddle-full of liquor. Soon he became quite drunk and quite full of himself.

The little beetle found a dunghill left by one of the donkeys and clambered to the top. As it was still fresh and moist, it gave way to his weight just the slightest bit. But because he was drunk, to him the whole earth seemed to heave and jostle when this happened. And so, thinking that he had caused the earth to move, the beetle exclaimed, "Hah! I am so mighty that the world cannot support me!"

Just then a breeze shook the nearby trees and made their leaves clatter loudly. "Ahah!" pronounced the beetle, "the trees have seen me make the earth move and now they shake with fear!"

A few seconds later a cloud covered the sun. The beetle looked up at the sky and exclaimed, "Even the sun fears me and has decided to hide!" And so, the little beetle stood atop his mound of dung, surveying the countryside around him. He felt very important indeed!

Soon after, an elephant came into the clearing, but smelling the foul odor of the dung, he quickly retreated back to the forest. Seeing him run away, the beetle said to himself, "Why, I am so terribly mighty even elephants run from me! That big fellow is trying to escape with his life! At last, here is the chance I've waited for to really prove

myself! I will challenge the elephant to a battle!"

So the tiny dung beetle shouted, "Hello! Hello elephant! Come back and face me! I say a hero must challenge a hero! There is no hiding from me! I myself have just made the earth move, the trees shake, and the sun hide! Let all the beasts and gods see who is the greater of us two!"

The elephant stopped and turned when he heard the little beetle's taunts. He spread his ears wide as he searched for the voice. When he saw it was just a little dung beetle atop a pile of dung, the elephant approached, looked down and said, "Oh beetle! You cannot believe that I fear you! I ran because this place smells so bad! Don't you realize that I can win a contest with you so easily I don't even need to use my tusks, trunk, or feet to do it?"

But the beetle did not listen. As he shouted yet another taunt at the elephant, the elephant dropped a great mass of dung; the beetle's voice was snuffed out! Then the elephant turned and hastened back into the forest, trumpeting his regal call.

One who accumulates billions
And is unable to give it away
Will be ever poor in the world.

Castles of Sand

Along the banks of a wide, lazy river, a number of children were playing on a lovely beach in the afternoon sunshine. These were ancient times, but the same story could be told now, whenever children enjoy the irresistible magic of water and sand. On this particular day, castles quickly sprouted across the length of the shoreline beneath busy hands. And the longer each child attended to his or her castle, the more carefully each guarded it and felt a need to keep it separate from their neighbors'. Soon, there was no mistaking which castle and which territory belonged to whom.

But eventually, as it often happens, a child slips or falls clumsily upon a neighboring castle; or someone makes a comparison between castles; or a child acquires a special stick or shell to ornament her fortress and so it stands more proudly than any others do. On this day, when such a mistake was made, an insult was carelessly tossed about, and the insulted child ran up and stomped upon the offender's castle. The lord of the newly wrecked castle pulled the attacker's hair and shouted for the others to help administer justice. The boy was soon chased from the beach and given a kick or two for good measure! Then the children returned to expanding their own castles and provinces, each saying, "Don't touch! Hey, look at my castle! Mine is the best! Mine is the biggest!"

A short time later, the sun began to set. Dusk arrived and the children knew they were expected home for supper. Suddenly, it seemed as if no one had ever cared about castles. Squeals of joy were heard in the delight of destroying the day's work: some kicked their castles apart, others dissolved them with buckets of water. Then, one and all turned towards home and left.

In the quiet, only the pleasant lapping of the river against the shore was heard. And nightlong, the river gently smoothed the sand again.

May all beings be happy and secure;
May they all be content.

The Mice who Taught the Monk to Smile

 Around eight hundred years ago in Tibet, lived a cranky, ancient monk. He was a peaceful man, but not a happy man. It was as if a cloud of gloom continuously rained upon him; after many years his face became deeply chiseled with a sour scowl. Mostly he kept to himself, living as a hermit alone in a cold and desolate cave. From his mountain perch he contemplated the world below. But sadly, the more he thought about the world beyond his cave—the senseless wars, the poor or sick—the more it hardened his heart. The more he thought over the suffering that all creatures endured, the more fixed his frown.

Occasionally, when the old monk begged for meals in a nearby village, he would meet up with fellow brothers. The other monks reminded him that the Buddha was cheerful and content. "Don't you remember?" they pleaded. "Buddha said that life is as quick and changeable as a dream! If you're always this serious, it'll be gone before you've ever enjoyed a minute!"

But the miserable monk responded, "Well, then it's all the *more* awful that we should suffer from a *dream*!" So saying, the monk returned to his gloomy meditations.

Sometime later, the monk appeared in the village especially glum. The other monks inquired, "What happened? Did someone die?"

"Well, is there anything that *doesn't*!" stammered the monk. He turned and trod slowly back to his humble cave.

But one day, while seated at the wooden table in his cave, something happened that changed the monk forever. As part of his religion, he created mandalas: beautiful, symbolic designs made from colored rice and semiprecious gems such as turquoise, garnet and tigereye. Just as the old monk was arranging the bright colors into a lovely pattern, a mouse appeared on the tabletop. It scampered directly over to the mound of rice and stones and tried to remove the largest piece of turquoise! But the gem was just too big for the mouse. It wouldn't budge.

"Furry little sir," the monk addressed the mouse, "tell me your purpose! That blue stone is not a morsel of food! Why do you trouble yourself so?" But the mouse continued in its determined challenge. "Oh, you are just like a person!" he whispered, watching the mouse with fascination. "We also like to gather more things than we can possibly use; then we fight wars over them. So beware the trouble you bring upon yourself!" he cautioned the mouse.

Soon the mouse scuttled back across the table and down the table leg. "It appears as if that mouse has listened to reason," the monk muttered to himself. But soon after, the mouse returned with another small accomplice. Working together, they managed to separate the large gem from the rice, push it over the edge of the table, and disappear with it.

Just then, watching the remarkable feat of the two little mice, the old monk's scowl broke. It began as a slight, yet irresistible, upwards pull at the corners of his mouth; it spread to a noticeable twinkle in his eyes; and at last his frown released into a full-blown grin—the first in many, many years. It seemed that even mice follow their heart's desire whether it makes sense or not! He whispered a small prayer, "May all creatures, large and small, near and far, have whatever they truly want!" The monk seemed to grasp something delightful about life that he had never understood before. And he silently thanked the two mice for what they had revealed.

A penniless man
Who will readily give whatever he has
Is said by the wise
To be the noblest and richest on earth.

The Monkey King: A Jataka Tale

 When the Buddha and his followers lived at Jetavana, a certain monk in the group was always upset—so much so that he could barely concentrate. When the Buddha asked him about it, the monk replied that he desired many things he couldn't have; thus, he never felt content. "Oh, monk," said the Buddha kindly, "these passions have been discarded even by monkeys. It is all the more important for one who lives the holy life to leave these feelings behind." And the Buddha recounted this old-world tale about the monkey king.

Once, in olden times, the Buddha came into the world as a monkey. He lived among the treetops of a remote jungle with a large family of monkeys. One day, a woodcutter came to this same jungle to fetch a good supply of logs for his family hearth. But when the woodcutter felled a large tree, he accidentally trapped the young monkey underneath as the tree dropped to the forest floor. When the woodcutter saw his surprise, he decided to bring the monkey home as a present to his king.

The bright monkey quickly tamed and was soon the favorite royal pet. The king let him run everywhere about the palace. So the monkey spent his days visiting the royal courts and kitchens, the guards' quarters, and all the other enterprises within. The monkey easily learned to imitate the manners of the royal retinue, the ministers, the guards, and even the cook who chased him from her kitchen. It was impossible not to laugh at the monkey's antics.

After a few years, the king requested that the woodcutter return to the palace. Then the king asked, "As a favor to this monkey who has pleased us so, would you bring him back to the jungle where he was captured? It would be kindest if we let him live out his years with fellow monkeys." So the woodcutter did as the king bid: he brought the monkey back to the very same spot in the very same jungle and released him.

At once, as soon as the woodcutter had left, a hundred monkeys surrounded the palace monkey, all asking questions at once. "Where have you been living this long time? Where did that man take you? Did you go on a great adventure? Why did he let you go free?" On and on the monkeys clamored, full of curiosity.

When they quieted down, the palace monkey recounted his tale. He told them all about the king's splendid palace and how he had entertained the king. He told them of the sumptuous feasts, the elegant dances, the noble ministers of the royal court, the king's fearsome army, and the dark dungeons.

"But then, how did you escape?" they wanted to know.

"I was such a good pet, and I amused them all so, that they felt badly keeping me from my home. The king decided to set me free again, so here I am!"

Now the monkeys were really excited. "Oh, tell us all about palace life!" they jumped and shouted. "Tell us about the ways of people! Tell us about the grand deeds of a king!" they insisted.

"No, you wouldn't want to know," cautioned the palace monkey. "You really won't like it."

But the monkeys would not let up until he agreed to show them what life was like for a king. So the palace monkey picked a monkey in the troop and said, "O.K. then, you be the king. Get up on this high rock and make it your throne. We will set to work and bring you the best fruit in the kingdom!"

So the monkey king sat upon his rock throne, surveying his kingdom and looking quite content. Soon a huge pile of delicious fruit surrounded him. After a time the king monkey began to feel distressed. "But I could never eat all this fruit, even in a whole year! And now there's nothing left for all of you to eat," lamented the monkey king.

"Of course you can't eat it all," said the palace monkey. "But that doesn't matter to a king. The point is that you eat whatever you want, but you must not give any of it away. You must always keep a large pile so that others know you are very rich and very powerful!" So the monkeys, wishing to be like men, brought even more fruit and stacked it even higher around their king.

"What else do we do?" asked the monkeys when there was no more fruit to be had.

"You must all come before the king and praise him in every way you can imagine." The monkeys liked this idea, so they tried it.

"Well, no wonder he is king!" pronounced one. "His coat glistens like water."

"His fur is as thick as deep grass!" boasted another.

"I've never seen such a strong and capable animal!" exclaimed a third monkey.

"No one is as wise and dignified as our king!" And so they gathered around their king and enjoyed themselves in flattering him.

"Enough of that," said the little palace monkey. "Now it's time to come *behind* the throne and say *terrible* things about the king."

The monkeys didn't like this idea at all and at first refused to do it. But the palace monkey persevered saying, "You have to try this if you want to learn the ways of people! See what it's like."

So the monkeys gathered behind the rock and whispered insults about the king.

"Have you noticed how old and confused the king seems lately?" asked a monkey.

"His eyes seem dull and he constantly forgets what he has said!" chuckled another.

"I think his fur is getting extremely thin; I think he might even be going bald in some very funny spots!" tittered a third.

"I've noticed that the king eats more like a *pig* than a monkey!" said a fourth and they all howled.

At last the insulted monkey king could stand it no longer. He jumped off his throne and ran after them through the trees. But the monkeys each escaped in a hundred different directions from the frustrated king. When the monkey king at last returned to his throne, his eyes widened in astonishment. All the fruit had vanished!

"Where is the fruit?" cried the king. "All my fruit is stolen!" he bellowed.

"Yes, it's a shame, but these things happen even to kings!" said the palace monkey. "Now, your guards must go find the thieves. That's what a king would do. And when the guards capture the thieves, they must be sentenced to death at once."

"*What?*" cried the monkey king. "You want me to *kill* them? Oh, how could such a terrible thing come to pass?" he wailed. And he covered his ears with his hands and wept.

"No more! No more!" cried all the monkeys. "We don't want to know *anything* else about the ways of people and kings!"

The palace monkey, the Former Buddha, then recited for them a little poem he had made up about life in the palace:

"'This gold is mine, this gold is mine!'
so they cry both night and day:
These foolish folk who live in splendor
never think about the holy way."

"And," said the Buddha, concluding his lesson, "the monkeys ran away from the rock throne and back up to the tree tops where they all lived happily ever after."

Therefore do not judge people:
Do not make assumptions about others.
A person is destroyed
By judging others.

Mr. Kitagaki

 One autumn day, the governor of Kyoto—a large city in Japan—decided to plan a visit to the wise Buddhist teacher, Keichu. As a matter of politics, the governor wanted this opportunity noticed throughout the city. So he and his councilors arranged for a sizeable retinue to travel to the temple where Keichu lived. It took quite a few days for all the arrangements to be made: fine kimonos had to be chosen, proper gifts needed purchasing, food had to be meticulously prepared, and so on. But finally, a long line of important persons took their place in a procession behind the governor. The cortege proudly made its way through the streets of Kyoto. Crowds respectfully lined the streets and bowed to their governor as he passed.

When the governor at last arrived at the steps of the temple, his calling card was carefully folded in silk. His personal attendant ran with the bundle to a monk waiting by the temple doors. The monk and attendant bowed to each other, and then the monk carried the bundle inside. There, it was unwrapped and the calling card presented to Keichu. In gilded letters it read: *The Honorable and Esteemed Mr. Kitagaki, the governor of Kyoto.*

"This man has no business with me!" gruffly exclaimed the teacher. He handed the card back to the monk. "Tell him to leave!" said Keichu as he returned to his studies.

The monk, trained not to interfere in such things, slowly bowed and reluctantly took the card from Keichu. He dreaded the task of delivering such a message to the pageant of people waiting outside. With a fixed gaze upon the ground, the monk trod timidly back to the governor. He returned the rewrapped bundle. The monk bowed deeply, not daring to look the governor in the eye. "I am so sorry for the inconvenience," said the monk meekly. "I know you have made a long journey to the temple, but I must return your card. My teacher said he has no business with you."

At first the governor seemed totally baffled. Murmurs of astonishment and horror could be heard from the procession behind. But the governor held the bundle a few moments, and suddenly his puzzled expression changed to a broad smile. He chuckled to himself and seemed to understand what needed to happen next. "Oh! Of course, my error!" said the governor to the monk. He pulled out a pen and crossed out the words *The Honorable and Esteemed governor of Kyoto.* Now the card simply read: *Mr. Kitagaki.* "Please go ask your teacher if he'll see me now, won't you?"

When Keichu read the card this time he exclaimed, "Oh, *Kitagaki* wants to see me? Well, I'd like to meet that fellow!" And Mr. Kitagaki was led right in.

Refrain from harsh speech;
Angry words rebound
Full of pain.

Great Joy the Ox: A Jataka Tale

 The Buddha told this story in response to some rough words spoken between two monks. He called together a large group in the monastery hall at Jetavana. "Monks and nuns," he addressed the assembly, "harsh words cause even animals unhappiness. Listen to this story of long-ago, when bitter words caused a farmer to lose his fortune."

In ancient times, the Future Buddha once came into the world as a bull. While still a young calf, he was given to a farmer as a gift. So delighted was the farmer that he called his calf Great Joy. He treated the bull like his own child, feeding him his best rice and richest milk. With such loving care, in no time at all Great Joy grew and grew to a mighty size. He was black as the night sky and glossy as the night's stars: as powerful as any ox ever born, yet obedient and docile as a lamb.

After years of tender care by the farmer, Great Joy felt an immense gratitude. He thought, "I have been raised by this farmer with loving kindness and much sacrifice. At times he has gone hungry to make sure I am well fed. And because of him, I am mighty and strong as no other. I have a sure plan to reward him for all that he has done!"

The next morning, while the farmer was brushing the night dirt off the bull, Great Joy spoke to him, "Master, I have a plan to repay your many years of caring for me."

The farmer stopped his brushing and gently laid his hand upon the bull's large head, "Great Joy, you already plough my fields and turn my well wheel. You haul my heavy loads to and from the village. You work unceasingly. There is no need to repay me, do not bother yourself with such matters."

But Great Joy was set upon his idea. "Master, please listen. I have a wonderful idea, which will make you instantly rich. You will be able to live out your days in ease, as a wealthy man! Travel to town today and find a merchant who owns a very large herd of ox. Make a bet with him for a thousand silver pieces that your bull is the mightiest in all India. Wager that tomorrow morning in the village square, your ox will draw a hundred carts loaded past the brim with rocks, stones, and gravel!"

"Oh, good friend," chided the farmer, "how can you possibly do that? What ox in all the world could pull a hundred loaded carts? It's never been done. The whole town will think I've gone mad."

But Great Joy persisted, "I have the strength and I will not let you down."

"But what if you *can't* pull such a load? A thousand silver pieces is all I own! If you lose, I will be a pauper!"

Great Joy was resolute. "I promise you, I won't let you down. I will not lose the wager; you will not lose your money!"

And so, the farmer did as the ox suggested. He journeyed to the village and seated himself in the town square where people made their business deals. At last he saw a rich fellow dressed in fine robes approaching. The farmer mustered his courage. He took a deep breath and boasted loudly so that all could hear, "Ahem, did you men know that

I am the owner of the strongest ox in the kingdom? I doubt there is a bull in the whole of India that compares to mine! In fact, my bull might be the largest *and* strongest in all the world!"

At this brag, a hush fell over the bustling crowd. All heads turned toward the farmer. Finally, the rich merchant broke the silence, "It is known throughout the land that *I*, sir, own an entire *herd* of the world's strongest oxen! And just what is so remarkable about your single bull?"

The farmer secretly realized he had snagged just the right man. He promptly responded, "I have a bull that can easily pull a hundred fully loaded carts!"

The merchant scoffed, "And where is such a bull to be found, in the land of fairies and dreams?"

"I keep him at home," said the farmer.

"Well, if you think so highly of him, make it a wager then," demanded the merchant.

"Certainly," agreed the farmer. "I'll bet you a thousand pieces of silver that my bull can move one hundred carts fully loaded with rocks, stones, and gravel. Have the carts ready and meet me here in the village square when the sun rises tomorrow morning."

The two shook hands on the deal and went to make their preparations. The next morning, well before it was light, the farmer fed Great Joy sweet milk and hay; he bathed and brushed him till glistening. He spoke soothing, kind words to Great Joy— just as he did every day. Finally, he placed a garland of flowers around the ox's neck. Great Joy knew the day had come to prove himself.

By dawn, the farmer had led Great Joy to the village square. Women, men, and children lined the street, all eager to see if the ox would lose the impossible bet. The farmer was astounded at the scene—never had he laid eyes upon so many carts! They were leashed one behind the other by thick ropes, gravel and stones piled high like a small mountain in each. If the farmer harbored any doubts before, he now felt certain to be the town fool for having believed the promise of a mere beast.

But Great Joy stepped nobly before the front cart and patiently waited to be harnessed. He looked magnificent. Indeed his shoulders stood higher and broader than any ox ever seen. People stared, awed at his mighty presence. Two men struggled to hoist the yoke upon his tall, wide back. Then they secured the long line of carts behind him.

The farmer stood nervously, anticipating his shame in front of the townsfolk. He clenched the leather goad in his hand, whispering to himself, "I cannot lose this wager. This ox has made me a promise but I am its master. I must make absolutely sure he pulls the carts. Aiiee! I have risked my life's savings on the promise of a mere beast!" The farmer lifted his goad and fiercely struck the back of Great Joy, shouting, "Now you beast, pull the carts! Pull! Pull you beast! Pull you rascal!"

But Great Joy was astonished at this treatment, "I'm not a rascal! I'm not a beast! He has never spoken to me like this! He has never taken a whip to me! I will *not* budge!" Great Joy ignored the whip's lashes and the harsh words of his friend. He planted his hooves like the roots of four Banyan trees and budged not an inch.

Straight away, the crowd began to howl and laugh at the farmer whose stubborn ox would not even listen! Again, the farmer lashed Great Joy and cursed him. But the ox stared straight ahead and disregarded the goad, the farmer, and the jeering crowd. Soon the crowd pelted both the farmer and the ox with mud and dung. The farmer, greatly ashamed, hung his head and gave to the merchant every last precious piece of silver. The merchant chuckled as the coins clinked into his hands. "Anytime you want to make another wager, please come and find me! What ox could possibly pull 100 loaded carts!" he guffawed.

Despondent and penniless, the farmer unharnessed Great Joy from the line of carts and led him home. Villagers followed him with taunts, rotten fruit, and mud. The farmer tethered the ox to a stake and retreated inside his home in an agony of grief. "I'm a pauper! It took me twenty years to earn that silver!" he wailed and moaned. When Great Joy heard the pained sobs coming from the house, he neared the window and asked the farmer what was wrong. "I have lost all my money because of you!" the farmer spat out bitterly. "You promised you wouldn't let me down!"

Great Joy replied, "Ah, but master, it was *you* who let *me* down! In all the time I have lived at your house, have I ever hurt anybody? Have I ever been clumsy or even broken a pot? No. I have taken children gently upon my back; I have let even the smallest of them lead me. I have always done exactly as you've asked."

"Yes, I suppose so," sniffed the farmer.

"Well, then why did you curse me and call me a rascal and a beast?"

"I, I guess I was afraid of losing all my money," whimpered the farmer.

"Well, go again to town and bet the merchant double the silver. We'll meet him in the square again tomorrow—just as the sun rises. But remember; do not speak to me harshly. Treat me kindly as you always have, and I will treat you as I always have!"

Hastily, the farmer went back to town, found the merchant, and made him a new offer. The merchant, laughing that he had never made money so easily, agreed to another wager.

At dawn next morning, the scene in the village square was a repeat of the day before: a hundred carts in one long line, each stacked high with rocks. Again, the streets filled with people to witness the contest. Great Joy was bathed and brushed anew with a fresh garland of flowers around his neck. He walked proudly beside the farmer to the front of the carts, but people joked and chatted, not taking the two very seriously. The heavy wooden yoke was lifted upon Great Joy's back and the ropes secured in place.

The farmer stood beside his ox and gently stroked his mighty shoulders. After a while he leaned over and spoke softly into the bull's ear, "Now then my fine fellow, my friend, pull the carts along!"

And with these words Great Joy seemed to swell in size. His muscles firmed and he leaned hard against the ropes until they tautened cart by cart, up to the hundredth. Then Great Joy leaned further still: he strained and pulled and finally took one step. On he pulled. He managed another step, and then another, and another, until the very last cart had turned its wheels. Step after step, step after step—each just slightly easier with momentum—Great Joy continued his effort until the end cart stood exactly where the first cart had started.

It was amazing! Cheers and hoots rang out, flowers and money were thrown at the bull and the farmer. Great Joy, glistening with sweat, stood nobly and proudly in place. The merchant shook his head in disbelief but paid over the two thousand silver coins. Children reached out to pet the ox—the mighty animal possessing such remarkable determination. There was much to celebrate. And before the morning's end, the farmer and his good companion, Great Joy, trotted down the dusty road back to home where they lived happily, and richly, ever after.

Thus the Buddha finished his lesson with the monks and nuns, saying again that harsh words please no one. And he spoke this verse in conclusion:

Speak only kind words; never be unkind.
For he who speaks gently, the ox moves the whole earth,
And brings him wealth for love.

If you speak deceptions,
Everything becomes a deception.
If you speak the truth,
Everything becomes the truth.

The Thief Within

 Many centuries ago, a young, novice monk traveled alone in the mountains of Tibet. He wandered about penniless, begging for a meager meal from time to time. One day, just as evening fell, he found himself on a bitterly cold mountain pass. But there, tucked in a high alpine meadow, he noticed a small home. He knocked upon the door. When it opened, a grizzled, ancient couple greeted him. They welcomed the young monk into their home, allowing him to escape the icy mountain wind. Because it is an honor to feed a monk, they cheerfully readied a wonderful supper for their guest.

At some point during the meal preparations, the old man went outside to herd his cattle into the night pasture, and the old woman went to fetch some water at the well. They left the young monk alone, tending the fire. But suddenly, shouts from the house echoed from cliff to cliff in the mountain meadow. "Thief, robber!" they heard the young monk shout. "Get out and never come back!" The monk created such a noisy tumult that the old man and woman hastened back as quickly as their old legs would run—pitchforks and hoes in hand to deal with the thief.

When they burst through the door, all they saw was the lone monk—flushed as a berry, running around the table, slapping his right hand, and cursing himself. On the table was an open tea container, with a few tea leaves scattered about. "Thief!" he admonished his right hand and held it high, "if I ever catch you trying to steal a little something again I will be rid of you!" The old couple looked at each other and chuckled at the young monk. They served him a fine supper and offered a warm place to rest for the evening. The monk bowed respectfully and thanked them for their generosity, but he wanted to resume his homeless life that very night. Before he left, however, the young monk pronounced that on that evening, in their house, he met his inner teacher from whom he would never again part. And he thanked the old couple and went on his way.

When no attachments
Hamper heart or mind,
When virtuousness is practiced
Peace to win,
Who so walks this path,
Shall gain mastery
And freedom.

The Prince and the Monster:
A Jataka Tale

Once, the community of monks told the Buddha of a certain brother in their midst who had given up all effort. He no longer kept the holy vows. When no one else could encourage him, the despairing brother was brought before the Buddha.

"Monk, is it true," asked the Buddha softly, "that you are no longer making an honest effort at the holy life?" The monk bowed his head in shame. Finally, the monk answered that it was indeed true, he had given up. The Buddha compassionately replied, "Brother, in former times, the wise and good won their heart's desire by dauntless effort and perseverance. Do not despair. So, too, shall you gain what you need if you exert yourself. Listen, now, to this story of old."

Once, in times past, the Future Buddha was born to the good King and Queen of Brahmadatta. The couple rejoiced at the birth of their son, the new prince, and celebrated with a sumptuous feast for all citizens of the kingdom. A long line of guests admired and praised the infant. Royal advisors and seers were called forth to determine the boy's bright future. Consulting the stars, they foretold that the boy would grow to be a courageous man, known far and wide for his skill with five different weapons. And thus he was named Prince Five-Weapons.

On his 16th birthday, the prince's parents again consulted their advisors and determined it was now time for the prince to begin his formal training. He was to travel to the far kingdom of Gandhara and study with the greatest weapons master in the world.

And so, early the following week, young Prince Five-Weapons eagerly set upon the road to Gandhara accompanied by a small, royal garrison. He tingled with anticipation, thrilled to learn the arts of defense from such a master. The party journeyed many days to reach his new home. They passed through dense jungles, ferried across rivers, and marched from sun up to sun down, until at last Prince Five-Weapons reached Gandhara.

From then on, each day, from dawn to dark, the young prince practiced with determined effort under the watchful master. At first light the prince shot a hundred arrows until he hit a hundred bull's-eyes. After that, he hurled his spear until it flew a hundred yards a hundred times. With a sword, he sparred against his teacher until he successfully parried one hundred thrusts. Lastly, Prince Five-Weapons wielded an immense club and pummeled a hundred pounds of hay to dust.

Weeks, then months, then years passed. The prince grew extraordinarily strong and able. Soon enough, the time arrived when the weapons master granted him permission to leave: Prince Five-Weapons was well prepared for any battle. But the master had some final words for the prince. "You have tirelessly trained for three years and have mastered the art of four different weapons. These skills alone will be enough to protect you in almost any situation. However, there is one weapon left," he continued. "It is the most important and powerful of all. But I cannot teach it to you. I cannot even tell you about it because it must always be discovered by oneself. Go now, go back to your home and your country. Help your parents rule the land peacefully. In a short time your chance will come to learn the last of the weapons."

So saying, he sent Prince Five-Weapons upon the road home. This time the prince traveled alone, so sure was he of his skills. But after only two days of walking, he came upon a roadblock of logs, guarded by two soldiers. "Young sir," they warned, "you cannot pass through here! The road beyond is the haunt of an awful, terrible ogre, the fearsome monster Sticky Hair! He attacks each and every traveler. He devours them from the inside out! No one is ever heard from again!"

But the Future Buddha, proud and confident as a lion, replied, "Oh, he won't attack me, sir! I am Prince Five-Weapons! I must reach my home far beyond these woods. And I am ready to battle any foe that tries to stop me, however large and frightening. Furthermore," he persisted, "it is my princely duty to secure this road for other travelers!" He wanted the chance to confront the monster now. "That Sticky Hair is wicked and his evil minutes are numbered!" he boasted. "Oh! How very sorry he will be for his bad ways after I am done with him!" Thus, brandishing his four weapons, the prince swaggered past the roadblock and entered the forest.

As Prince Five-Weapons marched onward, the leafless trees took on bent, sinister shapes. They seemed to reach out with fingers over the road, and more and more it was like walking through a darkened tunnel. But the prince was steadfast, brave, and determined. He did not even flinch. Soon however, he felt more than saw, an enormous shadow moving among the tree tops. It kept pace with him. A large branch snapped, and just as suddenly, the monster Sticky Hair crashed through the timber, ripping out trees and tossing them in the path of the prince. His head was as large as a mansion, his eyes were like tureens of fire, his tusks were bulbous as drums, and he had the beak of

a giant bird of prey! He had an immense, purple belly, but his palms and feet were inky black. Worst of all, he was covered from head to toe with shaggy, sticky, gooey hair.

"Halt!" the monster rasped. "You are now my prey!"

But the prince—steadfast, brave, and determined as a lion—replied, "Ogre, you are not so smart! I knew what I was about when I entered this forest! Think twice about harming me as you have so many others, for with this arrow steeped in poison I will slay you on the spot!" But the ogre did not stop his steady advance towards the prince. Having warned the ogre, the prince then lifted his bow, drew it back, and let fly an arrow straight at the ogre's heart.

But it only stuck fast to the ogre's hair and did not hurt him a bit. Then the prince let fly, one after another, his ninety-nine remaining arrows. All hung limply like jewelry from the ogre's shaggy coat! The ogre shook off every one of those arrows, making a great clatter. They dropped right at his feet. He lumbered yet closer to the prince.

But Prince Five-Weapons looked up at the towering ogre, shook his fist, and threatened him again. He lifted his spear and hurled it at the ogre. *Thud!* It stuck fast to the monster's hair. Still undaunted, but reaching only to the monster's knees, Prince Five-Weapons marched right up to that ogre and swung at him with his club. *Bop!* But the club also stuck fast to the monster's hair and didn't hurt him at all!

The prince was steadfast, brave, and determined as a lion. "Monster, you are no good and I am here to make you quit your wicked ways!" He drew his sword and lunged at the monster. The sword, sharp as it was, stuck to the monster's hair like a toothpick! It did not even scratch him!

Seeing that his four weapons were now stuck fast to the ogre's shaggy coat, the prince began to wonder what his fifth weapon—the most powerful—might be. The prince looked straight into the monster's eyes and exclaimed, "Well, ogre! I guess you have never heard of me before! I am Prince Five-weapons! When I entered this forest I cared not for my bow, sword, spear, or club. I took account only of myself. Now I am going to pound you into bits of dust so this road will be made safe for others!" The prince then swung at the monster with his right hand. His hand stuck fast to the ogre's shaggy hair. He punched him with his left hand, which also stuck. Now the prince struck at him with his right foot. There it stayed, stuck. And so he bravely kicked the monster with his left foot. It also stuck.

But Prince Five-Weapons was steadfast, brave, and determined! Undaunted, the prince shouted, "Monster, I will beat you using only my head! I will still pummel you to powder!" And so the prince, with all his might, butted the ogre with his head. But that also stuck to the ogre's shaggy, sticky hair.

Now the Future Buddha, the young Prince Five-Weapons, dangled from the ogre's body, held fast in five sticky places. But for all that, he was still unafraid. He thought to himself, "I have great faith in all that my master taught me . . . but I have little time left to discover the fifth weapon."

As for the ogre, he too began to wonder about the situation. "This is some lion of a youth, totally fearless like no other! For although he is trapped by a monster like me, he appears neither to tremble nor quake! He must have a secret weapon! I wonder if I'm risking my own life! For in all the time I have eaten travelers, I have never yet seen his match!"

The ogre grew alarmed. He hesitated before devouring the young prince. He asked, "Sir, why are you not afraid of me? Aren't all people afraid of monsters? Do you perhaps have a secret weapon?"

"Ogre, why should I be afraid?" asked Prince Five-Weapons. "For at some time in one's life death is absolutely certain." And so saying, the prince suddenly realized what his fifth weapon was. He proclaimed to the monster, "I do indeed have a secret weapon: it is the weapon of truth and good deeds! My secret weapon will tear at your insides like a sword for the harm you have wreaked! You will certainly perish along with me!"

Fearing for his life now, the monster trembled. He whispered to himself, "What this youth says must be true; his courage has not wavered! I couldn't digest a bite of this hero! Not even if he were smaller than a pea!" Terrified now with the fear of his own death, the Monster Sticky Hair delicately plucked the young prince from his gooey, shaggy fur and placed him back upon the road.

"Young prince, you are a lion among men! I will leave you be. Return to your kingdom, your family and friends. I am done with you."

But the prince marched right back up to that ogre. "I am not done with *you* monster! Having been so wicked, you must now change!" scolded the prince. "Don't you know the reason you are such a monster is that you harm others? You have gobbled up many a traveler. If you continue to do this, you will become even more monstrous! You will never have a friend in all eternity! From now on you must help and protect each traveler through your forest. If you do not make this change, I will be back again, right away, to set you straight!"

And so, Prince Five-Weapons, full of confidence, set off again towards his kingdom. The now timid monster accompanied him to the edge of the forest, where they bid goodbye. And the monster did indeed find that through helping one traveler after another, he became a happier and more comely creature. Others didn't flee in fright, and he made many new friends. People felt safe when they passed through the region, knowing they were protected from bandits and beasts. Sticky Hair tended his forest like a garden, and it too became more beautiful.

Prince Five-Weapons lived out his days exactly as the prophets foretold. He became a great and just ruler of his peaceful country. He was often compared to a lion—loved by all for being steadfast, brave, and determined.

Thus, the Buddha ended his lesson with the monks, reciting this verse about the undauntable Prince Five-Weapons who made his kingdom safe for all:

When no attachment
Hampers heart or mind,
When virtuousness is practiced
Peace to win,
Who so walks,
Shall gain mastery
And freedom.

Just like weeds
To the planted field—
The bane of us all
Is anger.

Perfecting Patience

 About a century ago, one of the most beloved Buddhist teachers in Tibet was a wandering monk named Patrul Rinpoche. Despite the fact that he was a learned scholar, he often dressed in rags as he wandered about the mountains, disguised even from his followers. He disregarded many of the trappings of religious practice and instead focused on the essence of spiritual life. Often he played the role of a trickster to make his point.

One time, Patrul Rinpoche wanted to pay a visit to a famous hermit, an old man who'd hidden for twenty years in a remote mountain cave. Patrul journeyed from one village to the next, asking for advice as to the hermit's whereabouts. Finally, a day's walk from any town, he spied some prayer flags marking the entrance to the cave. Patrul strode right in without any formalities, as if he'd long been expected for a visit. He stood silently, a wide grin on his sun-wrinkled face, while his eyes grew accustomed to the dark.

"Who are you?" issued a flat, deep voice from the back of the cave.

"Isn't *that* the big question all of us are trying to answer?" exclaimed Patrul. "Who are *you*?" he asked in return, still grinning. The old hermit didn't reply.

"Why are you here?" asked the deep voice again after a while.

"Ahah!" chuckled Patrul, "now you've hit the nail on the head! That's the *other* big question! Why are you here? Why am I here? Why you? Why me? Why any of us?" Patrul let out a large belly laugh at his own joke. It rang loudly throughout the cave.

Patrul then approached the meditating master and sat down across from him on the dirt floor. "Well, what's the view like from here?" he wondered as he made himself comfortable. "It's sure not much to speak of!" he exclaimed after a few moments. The hermit was doing his best to stay unaffected by this noisy visitor. His breathing remained steady and slow, his eyes remained shut. Patrul stared at him. "What are you thinking about over there?" Patrul finally asked.

"Sir," the old hermit replied in a voice not quite as deep or calm as before, "I am thinking of the same thing that I have contemplated for twenty odd years: patience." The hermit kept his eyes shut while he spoke. "I have lived in this cave by myself all that time. Here I meditate, I watch the days come and go, and I feel the seasons quietly turn. A person with less strength than I would grow restless with this slow pace of life. But with many years of effort behind me, I have perfected the noble art of patience."

"Oh, that's very wonderful," proclaimed Patrul. "Let me give it a try." He imitated the old hermit as best he could, matching his own breath with the hermit's steady, slow breath. Finally he closed his eyes as well. After some time, Patrul leaned over and tickled the old hermit gently in the ribs. "Hey! Psst." Patrul whispered, "What's your secret? This is boring!"

"Sir!" the hermit blurted, as his eyes opened wide, "why can't you leave me to my quiet retreat! Please leave my cave at once!"

"I will leave you if wish," Patrul replied, "but it looks as if your patience has left before me!"

There's a treasury full of jade and jewels:
It is in you.
Don't go searching
Far from home for it—it's here.

The Party

 Once the Buddha was meditating in the forest under a tree, just outside the city of Benares. On that particular day, a large party of thirty princes and their royal companions picnicked nearby. Several hours into the party, a number of the guests discovered that their money and jewelry had been stolen while they amused themselves swimming. When all the guests had been counted, they found one person missing—the obvious thief. Having had more than their fair share of liquor during lunch, the men grew quite rowdy and restless. With noisy debate, they determined to catch the thief at any cost.

Off they set in fury through the forest, crashing through the brush with bold threats of revenge upon the thief. Suddenly, they burst upon the spot where the Buddha quietly and peacefully sat.

"Have you seen anyone sneaking through these woods?" bellowed one of the princes; "There's a thief on the loose nearby!"

The Buddha didn't respond. Instead, he calmly inquired about their situation. One

after another breathlessly explained the story of the picnic, the jewels, the money, and the thief. As they retold their story, they worked themselves up to a frenzy again.

"Let's go!" cried a young man. "The thief is getting further and further away from here!"

"No one's going to get away with this!" shouted another, shaking his fist in the air.

But the Buddha suddenly interrupted the growing brawl, "What do you suppose young men? What do you think? Which is better for you?" the Buddha inquired. "To search after a thief and a few jewels, or to search after yourselves? Is there not a jewel within that you should attend to?"

The young princes stammered and looked sheepishly about. A hush fell over the group as they thought over the Buddha's words. Then one of the princes bowed slowly and respectfully toward the Buddha and whispered, "Thank you, sir." He turned around and the others followed close behind him, back to the picnic ground, and then quietly homeward.

Pay attention to your mind:
It is subtle and difficult to perceive.
Thoughts wander wherever they please.
The mind, well-directed
Will bring happiness.

The Art of Attention

 Matajuro was a Japanese boy who wanted very much to learn swords-manship. He thought he should start with the best, so he sought out the greatest swordsman in the land: Master Banzo. Many approached the famous swordsman, but Banzo didn't easily agree to take on apprentices. One had to prove oneself.

When the boy met Banzo, he knelt down and bowed deeply, his head touching the floor. Matajuro begged him, "Sir, I want very much to learn from you. I will dedicate my life to it. Tell me, how long does it take to become perfectly skilled in the arts of the sword?"

"A lifetime," was Banzo's stark answer.

The boy was astonished, but he pressed on. "Well, what if I work *extra* hard at it? How long will it take me then?"

"Ten years," replied Banzo.

Now the boy felt encouraged. "Sir, my parents are getting elderly, and soon I will need to support them. How long would it take me if I agreed to be your servant and studied with you day and night?"

"Seventy years," replied Banzo.

"But sir!" exclaimed the boy in shock, "first you say ten years, then when I say I am willing to devote my life, you say seventy years! How can that be?"

"Anyone in such a hurry never learns well," flatly stated the master.

"Very well then," sighed Matajuro, resigned, "I agree to be your apprentice and servant, no matter how long it takes. I want to be a great swordsman." And so, Matajuro began his apprenticeship.

As the very first training task, Banzo ordered the boy never to speak of swordsmanship again. The second task was to perform all of Banzo's chores. These included fetching water from the well, chopping a daily supply of firewood, preparing all meals, washing and mending clothes, and keeping the wood polished about the master's house. Month after month after month, this routine never altered. After what seemed a very long year to poor Matajuro, he hadn't even touched a sword, no less had any chance to practice thrusting or defense.

A year later, the situation remained unchanged. The boy was despondent. As he scrubbed a kimono in the nearby river, he made a decision. He would give up the apprenticeship before the week was over. While he daydreamed beside the riverbank, half-attentive to his chores, *thwack!* Banzo had quietly walked up behind Matajuro and landed a surprising slap on his shoulder with a wooden sword.

The next day, right after Matajuro had strolled thoughtlessly by, *thwack!* Out shot Banzo from behind a fence, striking the boy on the other shoulder. Later that day, as Matajuro prepared dinner over a fire, he sensed that Banzo was nearby, waiting for just the moment to attempt a surprise. Matajuro readied himself, holding on to a simple pot lid as a shield, just in case. But no attack came until later, when the boy had just begun

141

to relax for the evening, sipping some warm tea by the fire. *Thwack!* The wooden sword struck him squarely on the head.

As you can imagine, this new situation forced Matajuro to become ever more attentive: never sure when—or from where—the master swordsman would launch a surprise attack. Needless to say, the boy realized he was right in the thick of his training now. He found himself deflecting blows with whatever he had at hand—a piece of firewood, a kitchen ladle, a mop, a soup tureen. Matajuro got better and better at it, always alert and mindful of his surroundings. Not a minute passed when Matajuro didn't anticipate something unexpected.

Finally, the day came when Banzo could no longer land a blow on Matajuro, even by surprise. And when that day arrived, Banzo and Matajuro smiled knowingly at each other. They both realized that Matajuro would be Japan's next master swordsman by the time he got his hands on a real sword.

Do not be led by hearsay,
Test all things for yourself.

The Scared Little Rabbit: A Jataka Tale

 When the Buddha lived in Jetavana, numbers of holy men from various regions also made their home there. Many of these men practiced punishing religious rituals: some made beds of thorns, some ate and drank nothing but air, and some burnt their bodies with fire.

"Is there any value in these things?" Buddha's followers wanted to know.

The Buddha replied with mild amusement, "There is no more worth in these things than the noise that scared the hare, who then frightened the other hares, who next frightened all the creatures in the jungle, until one and all nearly perished." And the Buddha then told this story of long ago.

In India of times past, the Future Buddha was reborn as a magnificent golden lion who made its home in the jungle. Just down river from the lion lived a little hare that made its little home in a grove of coconut and fruit trees beside the ocean.

One day, returning to its burrow after foraging, the hare lay down to rest in the shade and protection of the surrounding trees. A warm breeze blew off the ocean, making the coconut palms rustle soothingly. The tropical flowers gave off a rich fragrance in the heat. The hare felt quite relaxed and content. But just before slipping off to sleep, he had a disturbing thought, "If this earth were ever destroyed, what would become of little me?" Ah, but the grass felt so cozy, the cicadas in the leaves chirred rhythmically, and before the rabbit knew it he fell asleep.

Not a minute later, a sharp crack broke the silence and a large coconut fell, landing with a loud thud directly behind the hare. The hare startled from his sleep. In his confusion, his last thought before sleep now became his first upon awakening; "The earth *is* being destroyed! It is caving in! I must run for my life!" Without so much as a quick look back, he ran so fast his long ears flattened backwards in the wind. His front paws could barely keep ahead of his hind paws.

As he zoomed by, fearing for his life, another little hare saw him and shouted, "Why are you so scared? What terrible thing are you running from?"

But the first little hare would not stop or pause, so the second hare ran after him, asking again and again, "Tell me what is it? What are you running from? Should I come too?"

"It's too frightening to tell!" panted the first hare on the run.

But the second hare pursued him and begged until, at last, the first revealed, "I heard the earth caving in! Run for your life!" And together they ran, one upon the tail of the other.

In this same way, a third hare noticed the first two streak by, shouting, "Run! Run for your life! The earth is caving in!" And she too took chase behind them. A fourth hare saw the other three run for all they were worth and so joined them, until finally there were a thousand little hares running in a panic, looking like a great, lumpy, white

145

blanket moving across the land.

And as the rabbits raced across jungle and plain, many other creatures joined them. The rapid padding of a thousand little paws passed by a wild boar snoozing in the sun. She startled awake, "Where are you going little sisters and brothers? What awful beast are you running from?"

"The earth is caving in, save yourself! Get your family and run!" advised the hares.

So the boar rounded up her piglets, her brothers and sisters, her parents and grand-parents, the piglets of brothers and sisters, and the whole lot followed right behind the hares. Even the hippos, half buried in muddy ponds, heard the ruckus through the jungle and lumbered up to the shore to see what was wrong. "The earth is caving in!" squealed a young piglet. "Follow us if you want to live!" And in this same way, all the small and large beasts of the jungle joined the great mass of animals on the run. Mice ran alongside elephants, geese flew alongside tigers, all kicking up an immense cloud of dust as they tore through the jungle.

But among those living in that jungled territory was the wise lion, the Future Buddha. When he saw the dust storm rise through the trees he quickly went to investigate. A seagull squawked, admonishing the lion, "Don't just stand there! Run for your life, the earth is caving in!"

Upon hearing this news, the lion thoughtfully considered it; "Surely the earth could not break up or come to an end! They must have heard or seen something they simply didn't understand!" But as he stood in thought, he saw that the animals were stamped-ing straight towards an ocean cliff in the distance. And suddenly, the lion was certain that if he didn't act quickly, every last one would perish.

The lion ran with all his force of speed to the foot of a hill which lay directly in the path of the animals. Three times he fiercely roared until the animals abruptly stopped and huddled together in fear. Calmly walking among them, the lion inquired, "Why do you run so? From what are you fleeing? Don't you see you are headed towards peril?"

"We are *running* from peril!" snapped a monkey. "We are running because the earth is caving in *behind* us!"

"But who among you saw it caving in?" the lion asked, looking around the group.

"Ask the elephants, they know," squawked a parrot.

An elephant spoke right up, "Well, we didn't see it with our own eyes, but the tigers told us and we believed them. They're not afraid of much!"

"Oh no," exclaimed a tiger, "It wasn't us who saw the earth cave in. We heard about it from an eagle! Eagles can see things at a great distance, and she told us to run for our lives!"

"I don't know who first saw the earth breaking up," objected the eagle. "From above I spied the group running through the jungle and I swooped down to ask what was the matter. It was the wild boars who told me about it!"

The boars shook their grisly heads in protest, "Well, the little hares know all about it; they were the first ones running!"

After each hare was questioned, the first little hare, the one who lived among the coconut trees, was at last found.

So the lion asked, "Friend, could this be true that the earth is caving in? What did you see?"

"Well," the hare timidly replied, "I didn't see it so much as I heard it and I felt it too!"

"Oh, and precisely what did you hear?" queried the lion.

"I was just about to fall asleep beside my burrow when I had a terrible thought, 'What would become of little me if the earth ever gave way and caved in?' Just at that instant I heard the sound of the earth caving in—right behind me—so I ran away as fast as I could."

And the great lion guessed right away the hare's mistake. "Come, upon my back little friend and show me your home. Together we will look and see if the earth is coming to an end." The gentle lion, the Former Buddha, reassured all the creatures that he would return quickly. He requested that they stay put, right at the base of the hill.

Swiftly the two sped away, the hare upon the lion's back. The hare directed the lion to the grove of trees. But the little hare, greatly alarmed, jumped right off the lion's back when they got too near to the burrow. "I dare not go an inch further!" peeped the frightened little hare. "This is too close to where I heard the earth caving in."

"Very well, little friend," said the lion gently, "you stay right here and I'll go have a look." He walked through the trees in the direction of the burrow. Soon, the lion came upon a place where the grass was evenly matted. He knew it must have been the hare's resting spot. And right beside this place, just as the lion had anticipated, was the largest coconut he'd ever seen.

He went back to the little hare. "Come with me friend, don't be afraid," the lion coaxed. "I want you to see something." He directed the hare to the enormous coconut. "Can you guess what made the sound of the earth caving in?"

Seeing the huge coconut beside his nest for the first time, the hare knew he'd made a very big and very silly mistake. Together, the lion and hare swiftly returned to the waiting animals and told the truth. Some laughed at the hare's foolish blunder; some were angered at the distress it had caused them. But all were greatly relieved nonetheless, for if the Future Buddha had not come to their aid, surely they would have continued over the next hill and over a cliff to their deaths. And so their lives were saved at the last minute, but they also learned an important lesson about hearsay and rumor that they never again forgot.

And thus the Buddha concluded his lesson saying, "My good brothers and sisters, never be led by hearsay; test all things for yourself."

Sources of Quotes & Sayings

Page v

"Half of the holy life, Buddha, is good and noble friends, companionship and association with the good." / "Not so, Ananda; all of holy life is friendship, companionship and association with the good." From the <u>Samyutta Nikaya</u>, translated by John Ireland.

Page ix

"My true religion is kindness." This quote from the present-day Dalai Lama, the 14th, can be found in <u>Lama: A Biography of the Tibetan Spiritual and Political Leader</u> by Demi. A nearly identical quote from the Dalai Lama can be found in Surya Das's <u>The Snow Lion's Turquoise Mane</u> and in Salzberg's <u>Lovingkindness: The Revolutionary Art of Happiness</u>.

Page 2

"If you speak delusions, everything becomes a delusion; / If you speak the truth, everything becomes the truth. / Outside the truth there is no delusion, / But outside delusion there is no special truth. / Followers of Buddha's Way! / Why do you so earnestly seek the truth in distant places? / Look for delusion and truth in the bottom of your own hearts." My version adapted from the above in <u>One Robe, One Bowl: The Zen Poetry of Ryokan</u>, John Stevens translator.

Page 6

"All fear death, / All hold life dear. / Feel for others / As you do for yourself; / Remember this / And cause no harm." Adapted from five different translations of the <u>Dhammapada</u>, Chapter 10, "Violence."

Page 11

"Rest in a natural way like a small child. / Rest like an ocean without waves. / Rest within clarity like a candle flame.

/ Rest without self-concerns like a human corpse. / Rest unmoving like a mountain." My version adapted from the above "Songs of Milarepa," translated by Karma Tsultrim Palmo, in <u>Entering the Stream: An Introduction to the Buddha and His Teachings</u>, Samual Bercholz and Sherab Chodzin Kohn, editors.

Page 16

"Delight in mindfulness / Notice your thoughts." Adapted from five different translations of the <u>Dhammapada</u>, Chapter 23, "The Elephant."

Page 20

"Getting or losing: how to tell which is which? / I lean here smiling softly to the breeze. / The spider so pleased with his artful web / Has netted only fallen petals, / Not a single bug to eat. / I lean here smiling softly to the breeze." "I Saw It I Wrote It," by Yuan Mei, in <u>I Don't Bow to Buddhas: Selected Poems of Yuan Mei</u>, translated from the Chinese and with an introduction by J.P. Seaton.

Page 24

"Let one's thoughts of boundless love / Pervade the whole world—/ Above, below and across without any obstruction, / Without any hatred, without enmity." Adapted from a number of translations of the "Metta-sutta," or the "Discourse on Universal Love." In the <u>Suttanipata</u>, Pali Text Society.

Page 29

"Whatever harm / An enemy may do to you, / Your own thoughts, stormy and uncontrolled, / Will harm you more." Adapted from five different translations of the <u>Dhammapada</u>, Chapter 3, "The Mind."

Page 32

"If you wish to see the truth, / then hold no opinions for or against anything. / To set up what you like against what you dislike is the disease of the mind." My version adapted from the above, found in <u>Verses on the Faith Mind by Seng-Tsan, the third Zen Patriarch</u>, translated by Richard B. Clarke.

Page 36

"It's good to be relaxed and go out to the people, / Really think about your work—and search for happiness, / A great path comes in front of you, and Heaven opens the gate; / And then? Do all you can for those who haven't what you have." My version adapted from the above, "#91, After the Gold" in <u>Kuan Yin: Myths and Revelations of the Chinese Goddess of Compassion</u>, Martin Palmer and Jay Ramsay with Man-Ho Kwok.

Page 40

"Thus shall you think / Of all this fleeting world: / A star at dawn, a bubble in a stream; / A flash of lightning in a summer cloud, / A flickering lamp, an illusion, a dream." From <u>The Diamond Sutra and the Sutra of Hui- Neng</u>, translated by A.F. Price.

Page 42

"When there is anger, offer loving kindness. / When there is selfishness, offer generosity. / When there is deceit, offer the truth." Adapted from five different translations of the <u>Dhammapada</u>, Chapter 17, "Anger."

Page 46

"Those who remain tranquil / When they perceive another's anger, / Protect themselves and all other beings."
Adapted from above saying in <u>The Tibetan Dhammapada</u>, Gareth Sparham, translator.

Page 49

"'I want this, I want that' / Is nothing but foolishness. / I'll tell you a secret—'All things are impermanent.'" From
<u>One Robe, One Bowl: The Zen Poetry of Ryokan</u>, translated by John Stevens.

Page 53

"We must all face death / Those who really know it / Put aside their quarrels." Adapted from five different
translations of the <u>Dhammapada</u>, Chapter 1, "The Twin Verses."

Page 60

"The sound of the stream / is, after all, / without a present, or a past. / The beauty of the mountain colors; / what
could it have to do / with 'right' or 'wrong'?" From <u>The Clouds Should Know Me by Now: Buddhist Poet
Monks of China</u>, edited by Red Pine and Mike O'Connor.

Page 64

"To be attached to a certain view, / To look down upon other views as inferior—/ This the wise call a hindrance."
My version adapted from the above in the <u>Suttanipata</u>, Pali Text Society.

Page 67

"Beyond the broken ground, go on to finish all that's to be done / Act on your intentions and nothing will be
wrong—/ A broad heart can encompass every imaginable thing,/ And things like this, seen from over you,
bring real blessing." My version adapted from the above, "#25, An Overview," in <u>Kuan Yin: Myths and Revelations of the Chinese Goddess of Compassion</u>, Martin Palmer and Jay Ramsay with Man-Ho Kwok.

Page 72

"Purify your heart; / There is no place to hide." "The Awakened," my adaptation from five different translations of
the <u>Dhammapada</u>. Adapted from five different translations of the <u>Dhammapada</u>, Chapter 14, "The Awakened."

Page 76

"For never in this world / Do hatreds cease through hatred; / Through love alone do they end. / This is the ancient
and eternal law." Adapted from five different translations of the <u>Dhammapada</u>, Chapter 1, "The Twin Verses."
This quote is also found in <u>Jataka</u> #371, the story of Prince Dhighavu.

Page 85

"Although we are here today, tomorrow cannot be guaranteed. Keep this in mind! Keep this in mind!" From <u>Chinul:
The Founder of the Korean Son Tradition</u>, translated by Hee-Sung Keel.

Page 88

"A fool is his own foe." Adapted from five different translations of the <u>Dhammapada</u>, Chapter 5, "The Fool."

Page 93

"One who accumulates billions / And is unable to give it away, / Is said by the wise / To be a man ever poor in the world." Adapted from the above verse in "Bodhisattva Surata's Discourse" in <u>A Treasury of Mahayana Sutras: Selections from the "Maharatnakuta" Sutra</u>, C.C. Garma Chang, editor.

Page 96

"May all beings be happy and secure; / May they all be content." From a number of translations of the "Metta-sutta," or the "Discourse on Universal Love." From the <u>Suttanipata</u>, Pali Text Society.

Page 100

"A penniless man / Who will readily give whatever he has / Is said by the wise / To be the noblest and richest on earth." Adapted from the above verse in "Bodhisattva Surata's Discourse" in <u>A Treasury of Mahayana Sutras: Selections from the "Maharatnakuta" Sutra</u>, C.C. Garma Chang, editor.

Page 107

"Therefore, do not be the judge of people; do not make assumptions about others. A person is destroyed by holding judgements about others." Adapted from the above saying from the <u>Anguttura Nikaya</u>, translated by F.L. Woodward and E. M. Hare.

Page 110

"Refrain from harsh speech; / Angry words rebound / Full of pain." Adapted from five different translations of the <u>Dhammapada</u>, Chapter 10, "Violence."

Page 119

"If you speak delusions, everything becomes a delusion; / If you speak the truth, everything becomes the truth. / Why do you so earnestly seek the truth in distant places? / Look for delusion and truth in the bottom of your own hearts." Adapted from the above poem by Ryokan in <u>One Robe, One Bowl: the Zen Poetry of Ryokan</u>, John Stevens, translator.

Page 122

"When no attachments / Hamper heart or mind, / When virtuousness is practiced / Peace to win, / Who so walks this path, / Shall gain mastery / And freedom." From the "Story of the Present," the ending verse of the story of Prince Five-Weapons in <u>Jataka</u>, #55, the "Pancavudha-jataka."

Page 131

"Just as the weeds are to the field / The bane (of us all) is anger. / For those without anger, therefore, a great result comes from giving." My version adapted from the above saying in <u>The Tibetan Dhammapada</u>, Gareth Sparham, translator.

Page 135

"There's a treasury full of jade and jewels: it is in you / Don't go searching far from home for it—it's here, / Or you're like the man with a lantern looking for light, / And can't you see what a total waste of time *that* is?" From, "#10, It's You," in <u>Kuan Yin: Myths and Revelations of the Chinese Goddess of Compassion</u>, Martin Palmer and Jay Ramsay with Man-Ho Kwok.

Page 139

"Pay attention to your mind: / It is subtle and difficult to perceive. Thoughts wander wherever they please. / The mind, well directed / Will bring happiness." Adapted from five different translations of the <u>Dhammapada</u>, Chapter 3, "Thought."

Page 143

"Now, look you Kalamas, do not be led by reports, or tradition, or hearsay. Be not led by the authority of religious texts, nor by mere logic or inference, nor by considering appearances, nor by the delight in speculative opinions, nor by seeming possibilities, nor by the idea: 'this is our teacher.' But, O Kalamas, when you know for yourselves that certain things are unwholesome and wrong, and bad, then give them up . . . And when you know for yourselves that certain things are wholesome and good, then accept them and follow them. My version adapted from the above discourse in the <u>Digha-Nikaya</u>, Nanavasa Thera, editor.

Story Sources

Birdsnest

Birdsnest is a quintessential Zen parable: a deceptively simple story combining humor and seriousness. Other stories about the monk Birdsnest can be found in several sources; Robert Aitken tells a version that enlists more audience participation in <u>Dharma Family Treasures</u>, edited by Sandy Eastoak. Rafe Martin, a renowned Buddhist storyteller, also briefly recounts this story of the tree-perching monk in his commentary section of <u>The Hungry Tigress</u>. What Birdsnest quotes is a verse from the <u>Dhammapada</u> in Chapter 14: "To Refrain from all evil and develop the wholesome, / To Purify one's mind, is what the Budhhas teach."

The Mustard Seed

The story of Kisa Gotami comprises one of the canonical teaching stories about death from early Theravadan Buddhism. The story of Kisa Gotami illustrates one of the four noble truths of Buddhism: that impermanence and *dukkha* is common to all humanity. A fairly direct translation can be read in E.W. Burlingame's <u>Buddhist Parables</u> indexed as #30, "Parables from Various Sources on Death." Other versions can also be found in Kornfield and Feldman's <u>Stories of the Spirit, Stories of the Heart</u>, as well as in Rafe Martin's <u>Hungry Tigress</u>.

The Elephant and the Wind

Jataka #105 is the original version of this story describing the frightened elephant. These stories first appeared as the <u>Jataka Stories of the Buddha's Former Births</u> in 1895, translated by the Pali Text Society of London and edited by E.B. Cowell. The original Jatakas can be a bit stilted and archaic owing to the fact they were passed down orally for hundreds of years. When they were at last "written" down, the stories were scratched into palm leaves before a true literary tradition existed. Another modernized version of this story, without the "Story of the Present," can be found as "Fearing the Wind" in Nancy DeRoin's <u>Fables from the Buddha</u>.

The Monk's Heavy Load

This is a popular teaching story about a Japanese Zen master, Tanzan, and his disciple Ekido; it can be found in many sources. One of the earlier sources of it in English is story #14 in Zen Flesh, Zen Bones complied by Paul Reps. It can also be found as "A Monk with Heavy Thoughts" in Heather Forest's Wisdom Tales from Around the World. Additionally, it is in Kornfield and Feldman's Stories of the Spirit, Stories of the Heart and as "Crossing a Stream" in Zen Koans by Gyomay M. Kubose.

When the Horse Runs Off

This allegorical story was written down many years ago China, although a close version is told in Tibet as well. It is based on a work entitled "The Old Man at the Fort" by the Chinese prince Liu An (178-122 B.C.E.) from his book Huai Nan Tzu. As we in the west say something is a blessing in disguise, a Chinese person might say, "The old man's horse is lost—how do we know that this is not fortunate?" Other versions of this story can be found in Heather Forest's Wisdom Tales from Around the World, Surya Das's The Snow Lion's Turquoise Mane, and in Chinese Fairy Tales and Fantasies by Moss Roberts.

The Noble Ibex

This story of the Former Buddha as a noble ibex can be found in multiple sources. Written in its archaic and oral style it can be found as Jataka number 483, the Sarabha-miga-Jataka in the classic collection of Jataka Stories of the Buddha's Former Birth edited by E.B. Cowell. It can also be found as the "Sarabha Deer" in Noor Inayat Khan's Twenty Jataka Tales. It is also a part of the Jatakamala: the collection of Jataka stories written during a high point in the Sanskrit literary tradition of ancient India. I know of no lovelier telling of this story than can be found in the ancient version, Once the Buddha Was a Monkey: Arya Sura's Jatakamala, translated by Peter Khoroche.

Heaven and Hell

This story illustrates that within some branches of Buddhism heaven is not other-worldly but is to be found in this very moment—when we are peaceful and without anger or desires. Another version of this classic Zen story can be found in Paul Reps' Zen Flesh, Zen Bones as story #57, "The Gates of Paradise." Rafe Martin also recounts a version entitled "The Zen Master and the samurai" in his book One Hand Clapping.

Many Elephants

This ancient story is still widely told in India today. A fairly direct translation from archaic texts can be read in Buddhist Parables, by E.W. Burlingame as story #22, "The Blind Men and Elephant." Heather Forest in her book, Wisdom Tales, retells a version inspired by the Sufi tradition. Children's picture book versions of this folktale include Seven Blind Mice by Ed Young and The Blind Men and the Elephant: An Old Tale from India by Lillian Fox Quigley.

The Worth of Cherry Blossoms

Another version of this touching story about Rengetsu the nun can be found as "The Cherry Blossoms" in Rafe Martin's One Hand Clapping: Zen Stories for all Ages. Anecdotes about Rengetsu, many of her poems, and pictures of her calligraphy and her pottery can be found in Lotus Moon: The Poetry of the Buddhist Nun Rengetsu, translated and introduced by John Stevens.

Span of Life

This short story about the Buddha is to be found in section 38 of The Sutra of 42 Sections. Another version of this story can be located in the Sutra of 42 Sections and Two Other Scriptures of the Mahayana School, translated from the Chinese by Chu Ch'an.

Teaching a Thief

This story has a classic Zen twist: a teacher that acts in a wholly unexpected way manages to effect the most memorable lesson. My re-telling of this story is based upon "Right and Wrong" or story #45 in Paul Reps's Zen Flesh, Zen Bones. It can also be found in Kornfield and Feldman's Stories of the Spirit, Stories of the Heart.

Anger

Another short story-lesson from section 8 of the Sutra of 42 Sections. A good source is the Sutra of 42 Sections and Two Other Scriptures of the Mahayana School, translated from the Chinese by Chu Ch'an. An expanded narrative of this story can also be found as "A Rude Man" in Prince Siddhartha by Jonathan Landaw.

Gifts for the Robber

Ryokan is one of the most beloved poets and monks of ancient Japan. More anecdotes about him as well as many of his poems can be found in One Robe, One Bowl: The Zen Poetry of Ryokan by John Stevens. This story is re-told in several other sources as well: as "Giving the Moon," in Heather Forest's Wisdom Tales from Around the World; as story #9, "The Moon Cannot Be Stolen," in Zen Flesh, Zen Bones compiled by Paul Reps; and in Kornfield and Feldman's Stories of the Spirit, Stories of the Heart

The Quarrelsome Quails

This story is one of the best known of the Jataka tales. It is Jataka #33, the "Sammodamana Jataka," from The Jataka Stories of the Buddha's Former Births, E.B. Cowell, translator and editor. Rafe Martin also includes a version entitled "The Wise Quail" in The Hungry Tigress. A shortened version appears as well in Heather Forest's book, Wisdom Tales from Around the World, as "A Flock of Birds."

Two Teachers and Tea

This anecdote is about Nan-in, the Zen master who lived in the Meiji era (1868-1912) in Japan. Other versions of this story can be found as "Cup of Tea" in Paul Reps's Zen Flesh, Zen Bones; in Zen Koans by Kubose; and as "Empty Cup Mind" in Heather Forest's Wisdom Tales from Around the World.

The Buddha and the Brahmins

This story about the Buddha can be found in the "Canki-sutta," #95, within the <u>Majjhima-nikaya</u>, Pali Text Society edition. Sutta or sutra means thread: it also means discourse or sermon. This sutta is part of the Theravadan canon. Another version of this story can be found on page two of <u>What the Buddha Taught</u> by Rahula Walpola.

The Broom Master

My story is a retelling of a legend titled "Greatness of Heart is What Counts," found in <u>The Snow Lion's Turquoise Mane</u>: <u>Wisdom Tales from Tibet</u> by Surya Das. Although we may never know if this story is totally true, it contains a poignant lesson of perseverance and faith.

The Old Teacher's Test

This story is a retelling of Jataka #305. As with all the Jataka tales, I begin as they do with a "Story of the Present": a problem that has cropped up for which the Buddha uses the older story to illustrate a point. This same story (but without the standard Jataka format) can be found as "The Wise Master" in Heather Forest's <u>Wisdom Tales from Around the World</u>; and as "The Master's Test" in Noor Inayat Kahn's <u>Twenty Jataka Tales</u>.

Prince Dhigavu

The story of Prince Dhigavu is part of the <u>Vinaya</u>, one of the canonical texts of Theravada Buddhism. The <u>Vinaya</u> is the "Book of Discipline": the first codification of the rules by which monks and nuns should live. Among the many methods the Buddha used to instruct—sermons, lectures, discourses, and dialogues—he apparently also used stories to great effect. Saddhatissa Thera edited the version of the <u>Vinaya</u> I used in this retelling of the heroic journey of Prince Dhigavu.

A Man, Two Tigers and a Strawberry

This story is an ancient anecdote, said to be originally told by the Buddha himself. Other versions of it can be found in <u>Zen Flesh, Zen Bones</u> by Paul Reps; in <u>One Hand Clapping</u> by Rafe Martin as "The Tigers and the Strawberry"; and as "The Wild Strawberry" in Heather Forest's <u>Wisdom Tales From Around the World.</u>

The Dung Beetle

This tale is Jataka #227, a story that illustrates the old adage, *pride goeth before a fall*. It can be found in <u>The Jataka Stories of the Buddha's Former Births</u> from the Pali Text Society, edited by E.B. Cowell; in <u>Buddhist Parables</u> by E.W. Burlingame as "Beetle and Elephant"; and also as "The Brave Beetle" in Nancy DeRoin's <u>Fables from the Buddha</u>.

Castles of Sand

I have retold this ancient anecdote originally composed as part of the <u>Yogacara Bhumi Sutra</u>, translated by Arthur Waley.

The Mouse that Taught the Monk to Smile

The story of the scowling monk is derived from a Tibetan tale about a Geshe (or monk) named Langri Thangpa. A shorter version of this tale can be found as "A Scowl Turns into a Smile" in The Snow Lion's Turquoise Mane by Surya Das.

The Monkey King

This story is Jataka #219 and can be found in numerous sources, including The Jataka Stories of the Buddha's Former Births from the Pali Text Society, edited by E.B. Cowell. The version I have retold follows the expanded tale called "The Wonders of Palace Life" in Nancy DeRoin's Fables from the Buddha.

Mr. Kitagaki

A much shorter version than my retelling of this Zen tale can be found in Zen Flesh, Zen Bones, by Paul Reps as "Calling Card." I have taken pleasant liberties in drawing out the drama and theme of this anecdote.

Great Joy the Ox

This is one of the best known of the Jataka tales, the "Nandivisala-Jataka," or Jataka #28, as it is translated in The Jataka Stories of the Buddha's Former Births, edited by E.B. Cowell. Another version of this story appears in Kornfield and Feldman's Stories of the Spirit, Stories of the Heart. A short version also appears as "Harsh Words" in Nancy DeRoin's Fables from the Buddha.

The Thief Within

Like the story earlier in this collection, "The Old Teacher's Test," all wisdom must begin with self-awareness of our own actions. Mindfulness is a fundamental theme in many schools of Buddhism—whether it be in meditation or in our daily actions. A shorter version than my retelling of this story, "Geshe Ben Steals," can be found in The Snow Lion's Turquoise Mane by Surya Das.

The Prince and the Monster

This story of the unstoppable Prince is Jataka #55. It can be located in several sources: in the complete collection of Jatakas compiled by E.B. Cowell entitled Jataka Stories of the Buddha's Former Births; in E.W. Burlingame's Buddhist Parables; and in Rafe Martin's The Hungry Tigress.

Perfecting Patience

Just as many Zen stories are similar to each other in their shock value and simplicity, stories from Tibet can be often characterized as tales of *crazy wisdom*—the unexpected route to an insight. A shorter version of this legend of the trickster monk, Patrul Rinpoche, can be located in Surya Das's The Snow Lion's Turquoise Mane.

The Party

A much shorter version of this story told about the Buddha can be located in the "Mahavagga" of the Vinaya, edited by Saddhatissa Thera. The Vinaya is the "Book of Discipline": the earliest extant codification of the rules by which monks and nuns should live.

The Art of Attention

This delightful Zen story can be located in more abbreviated form in Rafe Martin's <u>One Hand Clapping</u> as "The Art of Swordsmanship" and in Paul Rep's <u>Zen Flesh, Zen Bones</u> as "The Taste of Banzo's Sword."

The Scared Rabbit

This tale is Jataka #322. It can be found in <u>Buddhist Parables</u> by E.W. Burlingame as "A Buddhist Henny-Penny." It can also be found in the full collection of the Jataka tales such as <u>The Jataka Stories of the Buddha's Former Births</u> from the Pali Text Society. Rafe Martin has turned this one story into a children's book called <u>Foolish Rabbit's Big Mistake</u> and he includes it as well in his collection of stories <u>The Hungry Tigress</u> as "The Brave Lion and the Foolish Rabbit." It is also included in Noor Inayat Khan's collection of Jataka tales entitled <u>Twenty Jataka Tales</u>.

Further Resources for Children

Bancroft, Anne. The Buddhist World. Morristown, NJ: Silver Burdett Company, 1984.

Boisselier, Jean. The Wisdom of the Buddha. New York: Harry N. Abrams, Inc., 1994.

Chodzin, Sherab, and Alexandra Kohn. The Wisdom of the Crows and Other Buddhist Tales. Illust. Marie Cameron. Berkeley: Tricycle Press, 1997.

Demi. Buddha Stories. New York: Henry Holt and Company, 1997.

DeRoin, Nancy, Ed. Jataka Tales: Fables from the Buddha. Illust. Ellen Lanyow. Boston: Houghton Mifflin Co., 1975.

Eastoak, Sandy. Dharma Family Treasures: Sharing Mindfulness with Children. Berkeley: North Atlantic Books, 1994.

Forest, Heather. Wisdom Tales from Around the World. Little Rock, Arkansas: August House, 1996.

Horner, I.B., Trans. Ten Jataka Stories: Each Illustrating One of the Ten Paramita. London: Luzac and Co., 1957.

Jataka Tales. Berkeley: Dharma Publishing, 1989. Includes the titles: The Best of Friends, Courageous Captain, The Fish King's Power of Truth, Great Gift and the Wish Fulfilling Gem, Heart of Gold, The Hunter and the Quail, The Magic of Patience, The Parrot and the Fig Tree, The Power of a Promise, A Precious Life, The Rabbit in the Moon, The Rabbit Who Overcame Fear, The Value of Friends.

Khan, Noor Inayat. Twenty Jataka Tales. The Hague: East West Publications Fonds b.v., 1975.

Landaw, Jonathan. <u>Prince Siddhartha: the Story of the Buddha</u>. Illust. Janet Brooke. London: Wisdom Publications, 1984.

Martin, Rafe. <u>The Hungry Tigress: Buddhist Legends and Jataka Tales</u>. Berkeley: Parallax Press, 1990.

Martin, Rafe and Soares, Manuela. Morimoto, Junko, illustrator. <u>One Hand Clapping: Zen Stories for all Ages</u>. New York: Rizzoli, 1995.

Raimondo, Lois. <u>The Little Lama of Tibet</u>. New York : Scholastic Inc., 1994.

Roth, Susan L. <u>Buddha</u>. New York: Doubleday, 1994.

Snelling, John. <u>Buddhism</u>. New York: Bookwright, 1986.

<u>A Treasury of Wise Action: Jataka Tales of Compassion and Wisdom</u>. Berkeley: Dharma Publishing, 1993.

van de Wetering, Janwillem. <u>Little Owl: An Eightfold Buddhist Admonition</u>. Boston: Houghton Mifflin Company, 1978.

Vo-Dinh. <u>The Toad is the Emperor's Uncle: Animal Folktales from Viet-nam</u>. Garden City, New York: Doubleday & Company, 1970.

About the Author and Illustrator

Sarah Conover has long-standing interests in world religions and education. She has traveled worldwide producing numerous award-winning documentaries for PBS, the Discovery Channel and the United Nations. Ms. Conover received a BA in Religious Studies from the University of Colorado and an MFA in Creative Writing from Eastern Washington University. She presently teaches language arts at the secondary level in Spokane, Washington. Ms. Conover has been a student of Buddhism for over a decade.

Valerie Wahl currently lives and works in Spokane, Washington. She has read thousands of books to her children over the years, but this is her first try at illustrating one. She is a graduate of Washington State University where she studied Fine Art.